"Here We'll Have All The Time In The World."

His smile broadened. "And we can do *anything* you like."

The emphasis sent a shiver down her spine. Already her body had a few suggestions, mostly involving peeling those well-cut clothes off Vasco's ripped and tanned physique.

What was it about this guy that set her on fire? Maybe him being Nicky's father had something to do with it. There was already a bond between them, forged in blood, a connection with him that went far beyond their brief acquaintance.

"When you look out the window tomorrow and see the sunrise, you'll know you've come home." Vasco's voice startled her out of her thoughts. He looked at her, heavy lidded, over a sparkling glass of white wine.

"I'm not at all sure I'll be awake at sunrise."

"I could come rouse you." His eyes glittered.

"No thanks!" She said it too fast, and a little too loud. She needed to keep this man *out* of her bedroom.

Which might be a very serious challenge.

Dear Reader,

When I set out to write this book, I wasn't entirely sure where Vasco's kingdom would be. At first I thought of the Basque country of Northern Spain, with its fiercely proud culture. I even picked the name Vasco with this association. Shortly before I started writing, however, I took a trip to Barcelona. What an amazing city. It has everything—winding streets dating back to the Roman empire, Medieval palaces, grand Parisian-style avenues of elegant apartments, Gaudi's unique organic architecture, even a long stretch of beach!

I was especially enchanted by the Catalan culture of the area. The Catalan language has survived decades of repression and is thriving. To the uneducated ear (mine!) it's an intriguing mix of Spanish and French, and is utterly unique. Everywhere you go there's an infectious sense of the majesty and heritage of the people and their culture. I immediately knew that Vasco's nation would be a Catalan country, like the tiny nation of Andorra nestled in the Pyrenees mountains. Using creative license I kept the name Vasco because I liked it and thought it suited him!

I hope you enjoy Vasco and Stella's story, and enjoy your visit to the mythical nation of Montmajor.

Jen

JENNIFER LEWIS

CLAIMING HIS ROYAL HEIR

Harlequin®

Desire

ISBN-13: 978-0-373-73118-3

CLAIMING HIS ROYAL HEIR

www.Harlequin.com

Printed in U.S.A.

Books by Jennifer Lewis

Harlequin Desire

†*The Prince's Pregnant Bride* #2082
†*At His Majesty's Convenience* #2093
†*Claiming His Royal Heir* #2105

Silhouette Desire

The Boss's Demand #1812
Seduced for the Inheritance #1830
Black Sheep Billionaire #1847
Prince of Midtown #1891
**Millionaire's Secret Seduction* #1925
**In the Argentine's Bed* #1931
**The Heir's Scandalous Affair* #1938
The Maverick's Virgin Mistress #1977
The Desert Prince #1993
Bachelor's Bought Bride #2012

*The Hardcastle Progeny
†Royal Rebels

JENNIFER LEWIS

has been dreaming up stories for as long as she can remember and is thrilled to be able to share them with readers. She has lived on both sides of the Atlantic and worked in media and the arts before she grew bold enough to put pen to paper. Happily settled in England with her family, she would love to hear from readers at jen@jenlewis.com. Visit her website at www.jenlewis.com.

Dedication:

For Lilly,
my good friend and companion in many adventures.

Acknowledgements:

Many thanks to the lovely people who helped improve
this book while I was writing it: Anne, Jerri, Leeanne,
my agent Andrea and my editor Charles.

One

"Your son is my son." The strange man looked past her into the hallway, searching.

Stella Greco wanted to slam the front door in his face. At first she'd wondered if he was a strip-a-gram like the one her friend Meg hired for her surprise party two years ago. But the expression on this man's face was too serious. Tall, with unruly dark hair that curled around his collar, stern bronzed features and stone-gray eyes, he filled her doorway like a flash of lightning.

Now his words struck her like a harsh bolt. "What do you mean…your son?" Her mother lion instincts recoiled against him. "Who are you?"

"My name is Vasco de la Cruz Arellano y Montoya. But I go by Vasco Montoya when I'm abroad." A smile flickered at the corner of his wide, sensual mouth, but not enough to reassure her in any way. "May I come in?"

"No. I don't know you and I'm not in the habit of letting unknown men into my house." Fear crept up her spine. Her son didn't have a father. This man had no business here. Could she simply shut the door?

The sound of nursery-rhyme music wafted toward them, betraying the presence of her child in the house. Stella glanced behind her, wishing she could hide Nicky. "I have to go."

"Wait." He stepped forward. She started to push the door shut. "Please." His voice softened and he tilted his head. A lock of dark hair dipped into his eyes. "Perhaps we could go somewhere quiet to talk."

"That won't be possible." She couldn't leave Nicky, and she certainly didn't intend to bring him anywhere with this man. She prayed Nicky wouldn't come crawling down the hallway looking for her. Every maternal instinct she possessed still urged her to slam the door in this man's too-handsome face. But apparently she was too polite. And there was something about this strange man that made it hard. "Please leave."

"Your son…" He leaned in and she caught a whiff of musk mingled with leather from his battered black jacket. "My son…" his eyes flashed "…is heir to the throne of Montmajor."

He said it like a proclamation and she suspected she was supposed to fall down in surprise. She kept a firm hold on the door frame. "I don't care. This is my private home and if you don't leave I'll call the police." Her voice rose, betraying her fear. "Now go."

"He's blond." His brow furrowed as he looked over her shoulder again.

Stella spun around, horrified to see Nicky scooting along the floor with a huge grin on his face. "Ah goo."

"What did he say?" Vasco Montoya leaned in.

"Nothing. He's just making sounds." Why did people expect a barely one-year-old to be speaking in full sentences? She was getting tired of people asking why he couldn't talk properly yet. Every child developed at his own pace. "And it's none of your business, anyway."

"But it is." His eyes remained fixed on Nicky, his large frame casting a shadow that fell through the doorway.

"Why?" The question fell from her lips as a frightening possibility occurred to her.

"He's my son." He peered at her boy.

She swallowed. Her gut urged her to deny his claim. But she couldn't—not really. "What makes you think that?"

The intruder's gaze stayed riveted on Nicky. "The eyes, he has the eyes." Nicky stared back at him with those big gray eyes she'd tried to attribute to her maternal grandmother. Her own eyes were a tawny hazel.

Nicky suddenly darted past her, reached out a chubby hand and grabbed one of Vasco's fingers. The big man's face creased into a delighted smile. "It's a pleasure to make your acquaintance."

Stella had snatched Nicky back into the hallway and clutched him to her chest before she took a breath.

"Ga la la." Nicky greeted the man with a smile. Somehow that just made it worse.

"This is a gross invasion of my privacy. Of our privacy," Stella protested, clutching her son tighter. A horrible feeling in the pit of her stomach told her this really was the father of her son. She lowered her voice. "The sperm bank assured me that donor identity was confidential and that my information would never be shared with anyone."

His eyes met hers—ocean-gray and fierce. "When I was young and foolish I did a lot of things I now regret."

She knew Nicky had the right to contact his father once he came of age, but she'd been assured the father did not have the same rights.

"How did you find me?" She wanted her child to be hers alone, with no one else around to make demands and mess things up.

If this even was the father. How could he know?

He cocked his head. "A donation or two in the right pocket reveals most things." He had a slight accent, not a strong one but a subtle inflection warming his voice. He certainly had an old-world sense of entitlement and the importance of bribery.

"They gave you the names of the women who bought your samples?"

He nodded.

"They could have lied."

"I saw the actual records."

He could be lying right now. Why did he want Nicky? Her son wriggled against her, squawking to be put down, but she didn't dare release her grip.

"He might not be yours. I tried sperm from several donors." She clutched Nicky close. Now she was lying. She'd become pregnant the first cycle.

He lifted his chin. "I saw your records, too."

Her face heated. "This is outrageous. I could sue them."

"You could, but it doesn't change the one really important fact." He looked down at Nicky and his harsh gaze softened. "That's my son."

Tears sprang to her eyes. How could a perfectly ordinary day turn into a nightmare so fast?

"You must have fathered loads of children through the bank. Hundreds even. Go find the others." She grasped at straws.

"No others." He didn't take his eyes off Nicky. "This is the only one. Please may I come in? This is no conversation to have in the street." His tone was soft, respectful.

"I can't let you in. I don't truly have any idea who you are and you freely admit that you're here because of information you obtained illegally." She straightened her shoulders. Nicky wriggled and fussed in her arms.

"I regret my mistake and wish to make amends." His wide gray eyes implored her.

An odd tender feeling unfurled in her stomach. She shoved it back down. Who was this man to play on her feelings? With his looks, he was probably used to women rolling over every time he asked. Still, she couldn't seem to shut the door on him.

"What's his name?"

The stranger's question, asked with a tender half smile at Nicky, startled her.

She hesitated. Telling him Nicky's name would give him the right to call him by it. Almost an invitation. But what if he was Nicky's real donor? His father…the word made her quake deep inside. Did she have the right to drive him away?

"Can I see some ID?" She was stalling as much as anything. A man capable of paying for information could pay for fake ID. But she needed time to think.

He frowned, then reached into his back pocket and pulled out a money clip. He plucked a card from it. A

California driver's license. "I thought you were from Mont…" What was the name he'd said again?

"Montmajor. But I lived in the U.S. for a long time."

She peered at the picture. A slightly younger, less world-weary version of her visitor stared back. Vasco Montoya was indeed the name on the card.

Of course, you could buy driver's licenses on every street corner these days, so it didn't prove anything. She hadn't seen the donor's name at any time, so she still had no idea if Vasco Montoya was the man whose frozen semen she'd paid for.

It was all so…ugly. People had laughed when she told them how she planned to conceive her child. Then they'd frowned and clucked about turkey basters and told her to just go find a man. She'd wanted to avoid that complication. Frozen semen seemed safer at the time.

"Which sperm bank did you donate to?" Maybe he was bluffing.

He took his license back from her trembling fingers and shoved his money clip back in his pocket. "Westlake Cryobank."

She gulped. The right place. She hadn't told anyone, not even her best friend, where she went. Somehow that made the whole clinical procedure easier to forget. Now this tall, imposing male was here to shove it back in her face.

"I know you don't know me. I didn't know how to approach you other than to come in person and introduce myself." His expression was almost apologetic, accompanied by a Mediterranean hand gesture. "I'm sorry to shock you and I wish I could make this easier."

He shoved a hand through his dark hair. "You know my name. I've made my fortune in gemstone mining.

I have offices and employees all over the world." He pulled another card from his money clip. She took it with shaky fingers, which wasn't hard, since she still held Nicky clamped to her chest with the other arm.

Vasco Montoya, President
Catalan Mining Corporation

Catalan. The word struck her. She'd chosen her donor partly because he'd proudly proclaimed his Catalan ancestry. It seemed exotic and appealing, a taste of old Europe and a proud culture with a glorious literary history. She'd always been a sucker for that kind of thing.

And those eyes were unmistakable. The same slate-gray—with a hint of stormy ocean-blue—as her son's.

"I don't want to hurt you. I just want to know my son. As a mother, I'm sure you can imagine what it would be like to have your own child out there, walking around, and you've never met him." Again his gaze fixed on Nicky, and powerful emotion crossed his face. "You would feel like part of your heart, of your soul, is out there in the world, without you."

Her heart clenched. His words touched her and she recognized the truth in them. How could she deny her son the right to know his own father? Vasco's attitude had softened, along with his words. Her maternal instincts no longer screamed at her to shove him back down her steps. Instead she felt an equally powerful urge to help him. "You'd better come in."

Vasco closed the front door and followed Stella Greco down the hall and into a sunny living room with colorful toys scattered on the wood floor and on the plump beige sofa.

Strange emotions and sensations tightened his muscles. He'd come here from a sense of duty, keen to tie up a loose end that could cause succession problems in a future he didn't want to think about.

He'd wondered how much money she'd take to give him the child. Most people had their price, if it was high enough, and he knew he could promise the boy a good life in a loving environment.

Then those big gray eyes met his, wide with the innocent wonder of childhood. Something exploded in his chest at that moment. Recognition, at a gut level.

This was his son and already he felt a connection with him stronger than anything he'd ever experienced. She'd put the boy down and the toddler had crawled up to him. While his anxious mother watched, Vasco crouched and held out his finger again. His heart squeezed as the toddler took a tight hold of it.

"What's his name?" She never had answered his question.

"Nicholas Alexander. I call him Nicky." She said the words slowly, still reluctant to let him into their private world.

"Hello, Nicky." He couldn't help smiling as he said it.

"Hi." Nicky's grin showed two tiny white teeth.

"He said hi." Stella's face flushed. "He said a real word!"

"Of course he did. He's greeting his father." His chest swelled with pride. Though he could take no credit for Nicky other than providing half his DNA. Shame crept through him at the callous act of donating something as precious as the building blocks of life for a few dollars.

At the time he'd been glad to throw away the royal seed as he'd rather have died than dip into the royal coffers.

He glanced at Stella. He'd had his reasons for donating his sperm ten long years ago, but what were her reasons for buying it? His preliminary research told him Stella Greco worked at the local university library, restoring books. He'd expected a pinched spinster type, older and forbidding. What he found instead was a total surprise.

She was pretty, too pretty to need to purchase sperm at a store. Her hair was cut in a shiny, golden-brown bob. Freckles dotted her neat nose and her hazel eyes were wide and kind. He'd be surprised if she was even thirty, certainly not old enough to get desperate over her biological clock expiring. Did she perhaps have a husband who was infertile?

He glanced at her hand and was relieved to see no ring. He didn't need another person in the mix. "You must move to Montmajor with Nicky." Thoughts of paying her to give him the child seemed foolish, now. If he'd connected so forcefully with his own flesh and blood in only a few seconds, the maternal bond was not something that could be dissolved by any amount of cold cash.

"We're not moving anywhere." Still standing, she hugged herself. The living room of the little Arts and Crafts bungalow was small but pleasant. She wasn't rich. He could tell that from the simple furnishings and the tiny blue car parked outside.

"You'll have a comfortable home in the royal palace

and you'll want for nothing." The palace he loved with his soul, and that he'd once been cruelly driven from, was the perfect place. She'd know that once she saw it.

"I like California, thank you. I have a good job restoring rare books at the university, and I love our little house here. The schools are excellent and it's a nice, safe, friendly community for Nicky to grow up in. Believe me, I did a lot of research."

Vasco glanced around. Sure, the house was pleasant, but the sound of nearby traffic marred the peace and California was filled with temptations and traps for a young person. "Nicky would be far better off in the hills and fresh air of Montmajor. He'd have the best teachers."

"We're staying here, and that's final." She crossed her hands over her chest. She wasn't tall, maybe five foot five, but she had an air of authority and determination that amused and intrigued him. He could tell she had no intention whatsoever of changing her carefully thought-out plans.

Luckily, he had decades of experience in negotiation, and rarely failed. He could offer financial incentives or other temptations she'd be loath to resist. Although she might not have her price in purely financial terms, everyone had dreams and if he could tap into those she'd eventually be persuaded.

Or he could seduce her. Now that he'd seen her this possibility held tremendous appeal. Seduction offered the benefits of instant intimacy and unlimited enjoyment. Definitely something to consider.

But this wasn't the right time. His appearance was a shock and she needed a chance to digest the idea that her son's father would be involved in his life. He'd give her a day or two to accommodate herself to the new reality of his presence.

Then he'd return and entice her into his arms and his plans.

"I'll bid you adieu." He made a slight bow. "Please do some research into me." He gestured at his business card, held between his fingers. "You'll find that everything I've told you about myself is true."

She frowned, which caused her nose to wrinkle in a rather adorable way.

Stella blinked. She looked surprised that he'd chosen to leave without securing a deal. "Great."

"I'll be in touch to discuss matters further."

"Sure." She tucked a strand of hair behind her ear. Suspicion hovered in her eyes. He suspected she'd be locking all the doors and windows tonight. He had to admit that she seemed an excellent and protective mother to his child.

Little Nicky sat on the floor, engrossed in putting plastic rings onto a fat plastic stick. Emotion filled Vasco's chest at the sight of the sweet young boy that was his flesh and blood. "Nice to meet you, Nicky."

The toddler glanced up, obviously aware of his own name. "Ah goo."

Vasco grinned, and Nicky grinned back. He looked at Stella. "He's wonderful."

"I know." She couldn't help smiling, too. "He's the most precious thing in the world to me. I think you should know that."

"Trust me, I do. And I respect it." Which is why he intended to bring Stella back to Montmajor along with Nicky. A boy should be with his mother as well as his father.

As he fired up the engine of his bike, now hot from standing in the California sun outside Stella's house, he congratulated himself on a successful first encounter with his son's mother. She'd started by wanting to throw him out, and ended by giving him her phone number.

He gunned the engine and took off up the hill toward the Santa Monica freeway. A very promising start.

Stella bolted the door as soon as Vasco was gone. She wanted to let out a huge sigh of relief, but she couldn't. It wasn't over.

It wouldn't ever be over.

Her son's father—the one she never wanted or needed—had come into both of their lives and if he checked out after testing they'd never be the same again. The best she could hope for was that he'd go back to wherever he came from—Montmajor, was it? She'd never even heard of the place—and leave them in relative peace.

She wanted to believe that he was an impostor and that his country was the invention of an overactive imagination. He certainly looked like something out of a Hollywood movie with his worn leather jacket, faded jeans and scuffed leather boots. His looks were pure glam.

He didn't look like a king of anything at all, except maybe King of the Road. Especially since she'd seen him climb on a big, black motorbike right in front of her house. What kind of king went around on a hog?

Maybe he was a fake. Or some kind of crazy. California had enough of those.

Whoever he was, something told her he was Nicky's father. His hair was dark, almost black, and his skin tanned and scorched by the sun, but his eyes were unmistakably Nicky's. Slate-gray and intense, they'd surprised the nurses at the hospital who insisted a blond baby should have blue eyes. They'd never changed color and they were the first place she could read his mood.

Vasco's eyes were hooded by suspicious lids and dark lashes, while Nicky's still had the bold innocence of childhood, but they were the same eyes. Vasco Montoya was Nicky's father.

She settled Nicky into his high chair with some Cheerios and a cup of watered-down apple juice.

She hated that they'd had the whole conversation in front of him. How much could a one-year-old comprehend? Just because he didn't say much didn't mean he couldn't understand at least some of what was going on.

Two

A faint ray of sunlight snuck through the wall of miniblinds in the office of the customer relations manager at Westlake Cryobank. Stella watched the wand of light stretch across the neat gray desk toward the woman behind it. The finger of accusation?

Three days had passed since Vasco Montoya had appeared in her life, and she hadn't heard from him again. Maybe the whole thing was a dream—or rather, a nightmare—and nothing would come of it. She'd been preoccupied with "what ifs" and spent hours online reading about other people's experiences with absent fathers reappearing in their lives. Her brain was boggling with possibilities and problems, and now he'd vanished.

Still, she needed to know where she stood.

"As I said, madam. We assure confidentiality for

all our clients." The woman's voice was crisp and businesslike, her hair styled into a golden blond helmet.

"So how do you explain the arrival of this man on my doorstep?" She flung down the page she'd printed from a website on sapphire mining. An interview with Vasco Montoya, head of Catalan Mining and—as he'd claimed—king of the sovereign nation of Montmajor. Apparently he'd grown his business from a small mine in Colombia to an international concern with billions in assets. In the picture, he wore a pinstriped suit and a pleased expression. Why wouldn't he? He was the man who had everything.

Except her son.

The woman swallowed visibly, then shone a fake smile.

It's her, I can feel it. He probably seduced her into it. Rage swelled in her chest. "He knows where I live and that I used his donation. He wants us to move back to his country with him." The idea was laughable—except that it wasn't funny. "How much did he pay you?"

"It's not possible for him to obtain the information from us. All our records are kept in a secure, offsite location."

"I'm sure they're computerized, as well."

"Naturally, but…"

"I don't want to hear any *buts*. He said that he paid money to obtain the information, so you have a leak in your security somewhere."

"We take the greatest precautions and we have top-notch legal advice." Her words contained a veiled threat. Did they expect her to sue? That wouldn't help.

She sat back in the hard plastic chair. "I guess what I really want to know…" She thought of Nick, happily playing at the university day care. She'd hurried to Westlake after dropping him off early. "Does he have any rights, or did he sign those away when he donated the sperm?"

"Our donors do sign away all rights. They have no say in the child's future and no responsibility to support it."

"So I can tell this man that, legally, he's not my son's father."

"Of course."

Relief trickled through her. "Has he fathered any other children?"

"That information is confidential." The cool smile again. "However I can tell you that Mr. Montoya has pulled his donations and will not be doing further business with Westlake Cryobank."

"Why? And when did he do this?"

"Just last week. It's not unusual for a donor to find themselves in a new situation—married, for example—and to decide to withdraw themselves from our database."

"But how did he find my identity?"

She could hear her own breathing during the silence that followed.

Debbie English tapped on her keyboard for a minute, then leaned back in her chair. "Okay, I can't see there's any harm in telling you that you are the only one who used his sample."

"So if he hacked into your database…"

"Impossible." The woman's face resembled a finely made-up stone wall.

She drew in a breath. "Why was I the only one in ten years who used his sample?"

"We have a very large database. More than thirty thousand donors. Just glancing at his file, I can see that he's not American, and that he wrote in Catalan ancestry rather than checking a box for a more popular heritage. Those things alone might have turned buyers off. We advise our donors to…" Debbie English's voice trailed on and she remembered the excitement and confusion of her trip to Westlake Cryobank.

There it was again. His Catalan ancestry—unusual and intriguing to find in the prosaic database—had attracted her. Probably most people didn't even know what Catalan meant, or thought it was somewhere in China. She knew it was a unique culture with its own language and customs, a mixture of French and Spanish, charming and romantic with strong roots in a colorful past.

Just like Vasco Montoya.

"PACIFIC COLLEGE IN FUNDING CRISIS AFTER STATE SPENDING SLASHED."

The article headline caught Stella's eye as she marched past the newsstand on her way from the parking lot to the library. Rushed and scattered by her unsatisfactory visit to Westlake Cryobank, she had to stop and read it three times. She was sitting out in the garden on her swing seat while Nicky napped in the stroller after a walk. Three days had passed since Vasco Montoya had appeared in her life, and she'd heard nothing.

Pacific College was her employer.

She handed over some coins and scanned the article about a fifty percent cut in state spending on the small liberal arts college. Fifty percent? The college president was quoted saying that he planned to protest and also to raise money from the private sector, but that programs would have to be cut.

In her office, there was a message on her phone asking her to visit Human Resources at her earliest convenience. She sank into her chair and her breathing became shallow.

A knock on the door made her jump and she half expected to see Vasco Montoya respond to her murmured, "Come in."

"Hi, Stella." It was Roger Dales, dean of the fine arts department. Her boss. "I just want you to know how sorry I am."

"What do you mean, you're sorry."

"You haven't heard from HR?" He sounded surprised.

"I had an…outside appointment this morning. I just got in. I saw an article about funding cuts but I haven't had time to…" She hesitated, a sense of doom growing inside her. "Am I fired?"

He came into the room, a whiff of pipe smoke clinging to his tweed jacket, and closed the door behind him. "We've lost all funding for the books and prints archives. It's devastating news for all of us." He hesitated, and she saw the regret in his eyes. "I'm afraid your job has been eliminated."

Words rose to her lips, but not ones she'd want to say to a college dean. An odd fluttering, panicky sensation gripped her stomach.

"As Human Resources is no doubt about to tell you, you'll receive two weeks' pay and your benefits will continue until the end of the month. I'm sorry there isn't a better severance package but with the current financial situation…"

His words continued but her brain ceased to register them. Two weeks' pay? She had some savings but not enough to last more than six months, and that's if nothing went wrong with the car or their health or—

"If there's anything I can do, please don't hesitate to call me."

"Do you know of anyone looking for a rare book restorer?" Her voice had an edge that she hadn't planned. Jobs like this were scarce at the best of times.

"Perhaps you could approach some private libraries."

"Sure. I'll try that." She'd lose the university day care, too. Now she'd have to pay for child care or renovate precious and fragile items on her kitchen table while Nicky crawled around her feet.

Disbelief warred with shock and confusion as he opened the door and slipped from her office. How could her whole life fall apart so fast?

Stella spent three days sending out carefully composed résumés to every university library, museum and private library she could dig up on the internet. When one in Kalamazoo, Michigan, offered her an interview, she realized that even applying for a job with a very young child was challenging. She couldn't take him with her, but he was too young to leave for more than a few hours with even her most devoted friends. Her mom had died three years ago in a skiing accident, leaving her with no close family to count on.

"Maybe I should call Vasco and tell him I need him to babysit," she joked on the phone to her pal Karen, who sat for her occasionally during the day, but worked nights as a bartender in a downtown club, leaving her own three- and eight-year-olds with her mom.

"That would be one way to get rid of him. In my experience men lose interest in anything that involves changing diapers."

"Why didn't I think of that before? I should have invited him in and handed Nicky to him after a poop."

"Has he called?"

"No." She frowned. Now that he'd gone several days without calling, she was actually ticked off at him. Who was he to waltz into her life—and Nicky's—and announce his right to be there and then just disappear without a trace?

"Hmm. He did sound a bit too good to be true. Tall, dark, handsome, leather-clad and royal?"

"Trust me, none of those things appeal to me."

"Yes, I know. You prefer short, fickle redheads."

"Trevor had sandy hair, not red."

"Same diff, sweetie. Either way, he seems to have put you off men for good. Have you even dated since you guys broke up?"

"I don't have time for dating. I'm busy with Nicky." And work, she would have said until two days earlier. She'd been told, very gently, to collect her belongings immediately after her HR discussion. Apparently newly laid-off employees were not encouraged to mess with rare books.

"It's been nearly three years, Stell."

"I'm not interested. I have a very full life and the last thing I need is a man to screw it up for me."

"The right man will come along. Just don't be so busy slamming the door in his face that you don't recognize him when he does. Hey, look at it this way. Vasco already wants you to move to his country—that's a bit of a change from Trevor who wasn't even ready to live with you after eight years."

"Vasco wants Nicky to move to his country. He couldn't care less about me. Besides, he hasn't called. Maybe I'll never hear from him again." Annoying how his face had imprinted itself in her mind. She kept seeing those steel-gray eyes staring at her from everywhere.

"Oh, he'll call. I have a feeling." Karen laughed. "The question is, what will you say to him?"

Stella drew in a breath. "I'll let him spend time with Nicky if he wants, and let them get to know each other. It would probably be best for Nicky to have a relationship with his father."

"Aren't you worried he'll try to take over and tell you what to do?"

"He can't. He doesn't have any legal rights. I could tell him to go away at any time."

"He doesn't seem like the type who takes orders. But here's a thought, wouldn't a European royal have a large collection of old books that need fixing up? You might be able to find some nice work through him."

"Oh, stop. My job search is a disaster. Everything's so far away and the pay is dismal. Barely enough to pay for diapers, let alone support us both. Soon I'll be asking people if they'd like fries with that—hang on, there's someone at the door." The familiar chime sounded and the glass pane darkened as a large silhouette loomed outside.

Stella's stomach contracted. Although she couldn't

see much through the dimpled glass, she knew—every single part of her knew—that Vasco Montoya stood on her doorstep.

Three

Stella said goodbye to Karen and shoved the phone in her pocket. To her annoyance she found herself smoothing her hair as she walked up the hallway to the door. Ridiculous! Still, she might as well be civil since she'd decided that if he was Nicky's father she couldn't in good conscience try to keep him entirely out of Nicky's life.

She'd always wished for the kind of family you saw on TV, with the smiling mom and dad doting on their kids. Instead she had the awkward and hard to explain reality of a dad who had disappeared when she was a baby and never gotten in contact again. There'd always been a gap in her life, a thread of pathetic hope that he'd remember her—that he'd love her—and come back for her. When her mom died suddenly when Stella was in her twenties she'd even tried to look for him, until friends persuaded her that might bring more heartache rather than the resolution and affection she craved. They'd told her she was too nice, too anxious to please, too hopeful that she could put everything right and make everyone happy, when sometimes that wasn't possible.

Didn't stop her from trying, though, which was probably why she couldn't drive Vasco Montoya away without at least finding out the truth. Deep down she just wanted everyone to be happy.

She pulled open the door to find him standing there—even taller and more infuriatingly handsome than she remembered—his arms laden with wrapped gifts and a big spray of flowers.

"Hi, Stella." His mouth flashed a mischievous grin.

She blinked. "Hello, Vasco. Please come in." Mercifully she sounded calmer than she felt. What did he have in all those shiny packages?

"These are for you." His gray gaze met hers as he handed her the bouquet. Her heart jumped and she snatched them from him and turned down the hallway. The arrangement was beautiful—a mix of wildflowers and exotic lilies. The scent wafted to her. "I'll just put these in water."

"Where's Nicky?"

"He's upstairs having a nap. He'll wake up soon." She wanted him to know she wasn't going to disturb her son's routine for an unscheduled visit.

"That's fine. It gives us a chance to talk."

She filled a green glass vase with water and slid the flowers into it. Later she'd take the time to trim the stalks and arrange them. Right now her hands were shaking too much. "Would you like some…tea?"

It was impossible to imagine Vasco Montoya sipping tea. Swigging rum from an open bottle, maybe.

He smiled as if he found the idea amusing, too. "No, thanks." He unleashed the pile of packages onto the kitchen table, then pulled out a small rectangular present wrapped in dark red paper and ornamented with a slim white ribbon. "This is also for you."

She took the present from his outstretched hand, then realized she was frowning. Obviously he was trying to curry favor with her, which rubbed her the wrong way. "You shouldn't have."

"I've done a few things I shouldn't have." Humor danced in his eyes. "I'm trying to put that right. I appreciate your giving me the chance to try."

She softened a bit, more from his hopeful expression than his words. "Should I open it now?"

"Please do." He sat in a kitchen chair, apparently relaxed despite the strange situation.

Her hands shook a bit as she plucked at the ribbon and carefully pulled the wrapping paper off by lifting the tape. She was constitutionally unable to rip paper. Probably an occupational hazard.

The wrapping peeled back to reveal a black paper book jacket with an abstract picture. Her eyes widened as she realized that she now held in her hands a 1957 first edition of Jack Kerouac's Beat Generation classic *On the Road.*

"I know you like books."

"Where did you get this?" This edition retailed for nearly ten thousand dollars. In near-mint condition like this, possibly far more.

"A friend."

"I can't accept it. It's far too valuable." Still, she

couldn't help turning it over to look at the back, and peer inside. The pages were in such good condition, no yellowing or wear, that it must have been in a box for over fifty years.

"I insist. I like finding the right gifts for people."

She stared at him. How could he know about her interest in that era—music and art as well as literature— and that her life revolved around rare books?

His easy grin revealed that he knew he'd scored a hit. "I know you restore books, so I had to give you one in perfect condition or it would be like handing you work." He had dimples in his right cheek and chin when he smiled.

"How did you know what I do?"

He shrugged. "I searched for your name on Google."

"Oh." She'd done the same thing with his, which had informed her that not only was he the king of a tiny country in the Pyrenees, but that he'd amassed a fortune in the mining industry over the last ten years. At least he could afford the gift.

It seemed a shame to even touch the cover, when she knew how every fingerprint caused fabric and paper to deteriorate. Still, what was the point of a book if not to be looked at and enjoyed? "Thank you."

Still, there were a lot of unanswered questions, most of them hard to ask and undoubtedly awkward to answer. Like this one: "Would you be willing to take a paternity test?"

"Absolutely."

"Oh." For some reason she'd expected him to resist. "I found a lab locally. They said you and Nicky have to go in and they'll take swabs from your cheek."

"I'd be glad to." His expression was perfectly serious.

"Why did you donate your sperm?" She was on a roll now.

For once he looked uncomfortable. He leaned forward, frowned, shoved a tanned hand into his hair. "It's complicated. Mostly it had to do with being turned away from the land and family that meant everything to me, and finding myself here in the land of plenty without fifty dollars to my name. Not very heroic, huh?"

She shrugged. His honesty appealed to her. "I suspect money trouble is a pretty common reason. Most of the donors seemed to be college students. I guess it's a painless way to earn some extra cash."

"Sure, until you grow up and realize the consequences."

He regretted it now. Somehow that hurt. "Your donation has brought the greatest joy into my life. Don't wish that away."

He tilted his head, thoughtful. "You're right. Nicky was meant to be here. It's just a strange situation to find oneself in." A smile lit his eyes.

Stella's toes curled as a hot sensation unfurled in her belly. She wished he'd stop looking at her like that. As if he'd found the woman of his dreams, or something.

Definitely *or something*.

"I've decided that you and Nicky should visit Montmajor. Then you can see and decide for yourselves whether it's the right place for you to live." His easy pose and confident expression suggested that he already knew what their decision would be.

The urge to say no was flattened by the reality of her bleak economic prospects in California right now. "That sounds like a good idea."

His eyes widened. Apparently he'd expected at least

some resistance. "Fantastic. I'll arrange the flights. Is next week too soon to leave?"

Should she pretend she needed to "take time off work" or did he already know her job was gone? She didn't want to appear too much of a pushover. "Let me check my book."

She rose and walked into the living room, where she pretended to flip through her datebook, which was alarmingly empty. As she walked back into the kitchen his gaze drifted over her in a way that was both insolent and arousing and made her suck in her breath.

"After Wednesday would be fine. How long would you like us to visit for?"

He propped one ankle on his knee and his smile widened. "Forever would be ideal, but why don't we start with a month."

"I'm afraid I can't take a month away from work." Or at least from looking for a job. Even if he was paying for everything in his country she needed something to come back to.

Vasco's expression softened. "I know you lost your job at the university."

"How do you know that?" Suspicion pricked her. Was he behind it somehow?

He shrugged. "I called them to see if you were affected by the cuts. I'm sorry."

Her face heated. "Me, too. I need to find more work right away. I can't have a big gap on my résumé." He wasn't behind it. Local finances were. All the stress was making her paranoid.

"No need for any gap at all." He leaned forward. "The palace library has over ten thousand books, some of them so old they were handwritten by monks. As far as I know they have seen no restoration efforts in generations, so you will be amply supplied with work if you'd be kind enough to turn your attentions to them."

Funny how his speech could get so formal and princely sometimes.

"That does sound interesting." She tried to contain her excitement. It sounded like every book restorer's fantasy. Old libraries could contain gems that no one even knew existed. Visions of medieval manuscripts and elegant editions of, say, Dante's *Commedia* danced in her mind.

"You'd be well paid. Since I'm not familiar with the field you can set your own rate. Any supplies and equipment you need will be furnished."

"I'll bring my own tools," she said quickly, then realized she sounded a little too keen. "A month should give me time to assess the condition of the collection and plan preliminary repairs to those volumes most in need."

"Excellent." His dimples deepened.

Today Vasco wore faded jeans and black boots with a suit jacket and casual white shirt. He could have stepped right out of the pages in *GQ*. Stella became conscious of her less than scintillating ensemble of black yoga pants and a striped T-shirt that might well be stained with baby food. She resisted the urge to look down.

Besides, one set of eyes on her body was quite enough. Vasco's gaze heated her skin. Was he flirting with her? She was so out of practice she couldn't even tell. Trevor had scoffed at romantic overtures and seductive gestures, and she'd grown to think of them as childish.

But the way Vasco was looking at her right now felt

anything but infantile. "Glass of water?" She didn't know what else to say and the temperature in the room was becoming dangerously uncomfortable.

"Why not?" He raised a brow.

She busied herself filling a glass and was relieved to hear Nicky's voice rising in a plea for freedom from upstairs. "He's up."

At least now she wouldn't be alone with Vasco, and those penetrating gray eyes would have someone else to look at. Vasco stood up to come with her.

"Why don't you wait here?" She didn't want him upstairs in their personal space, knowing where Nicky's crib was. She didn't much like leaving him alone in the kitchen, either. Not because she had a bad feeling about him—at least not that she could put her finger on—but it was all way too much, too soon.

She'd committed to visiting his country for a month. Which gave her a queasy feeling of being swept away on a tide of destiny. For now, at least, she wanted to keep her feet—and Nicky's—firmly planted in their own little reality.

He was still standing as she left the room, possibly ready to go snooping through the opened mail on the sideboard or peering into her fridge and discovering that she'd eaten three out of the six Boston cream donuts inside it. She grabbed Nicky out of his crib and hurried back down as fast as she could.

The expression on Vasco's face when he saw Nicky almost melted her suspicious heart. Delight and wonder softened his hard features. Part of her wanted to clutch Nicky to her chest and protect him from this stranger who hoped to love her son like she did, and part of her wanted to put Nicky in Vasco's arms so he could experience the happiness she'd known since he came into her life.

She lowered Nicky to the floor, where he took off at a high-speed crawl.

"I think he's been awake for a while. He seems full of beans."

"Maybe he was listening in on our conversation." Vasco's eyes didn't leave Nicky. Apparently she was way less fascinating now that he was in the room.

Stella's stomach tightened. She'd actually agreed to head off to Montmajor with Nicky. "Will we stay in a hotel while we're there?"

"The royal palace has more than ample room. You'll have your own suite—your own wing, if you like—and plenty of privacy."

A palace. Somehow she hadn't thought of that part. A royal palace where Nicky might be heir to the throne. The whole idea made her feel nauseous. And Nicky's diaper smelled. "He needs changing."

Karen's idea of asking Vasco to change him crossed her mind but she quickly dismissed it. Far too intimate. She didn't want Vasco assuming fatherly duties, at least not until after the DNA test proved he was Nicky's father.

And she suspected he'd be willing and able to rise to that and any other challenge she could throw at him.

Vasco followed her into the dining room, where she had a changing mat on the floor. "When do they stop wearing those things?"

"It depends. When we were kids our moms would be trying to take them off already. These days it's common for kids to wear them until three or four. Everyone has a theory on what's right."

Vasco seemed like the kind of guy who'd let his kid run around naked outdoors and discover things the old-fashioned way. She'd probably try that if she didn't live in the corner lot on a busy street in full view of half the neighborhood. She wasn't sure they'd appreciate the view.

This thought reminded her how little she knew about Vasco and what his life in Montmajor was like. She'd seen plenty of pictures of him with his arm around different women on the internet, but no hard information about his personal life. "Are you married?"

He laughed. "No."

"Why not?" The question was bold, but she couldn't resist asking. He was old enough, over thirty, certainly. Wealthy, gorgeous and royal, Vasco Montoya must have women trailing him like stray cats after a fish truck.

His throaty chuckle made her belly tighten. "Maybe I'm not the marrying kind. What about you? Why aren't you married?"

His question heated her face. "Maybe I'm not the marrying kind either." It was hard to sound cool and hard-boiled while wiping a rosy bottom.

"You do seem like the marrying kind." His voice was soft, suggestive, even.

"Maybe I would be if I ever met the right man. I was engaged for a long time, but eventually I decided I was better off on my own."

She'd probably still be engaged to Trevor, still childless and living alone, if she hadn't made a clean break. It was an easy relationship, if not an exciting one.

"You're independent. Don't need a man to take care of you. I like that."

Don't I? The sudden evaporation of her income and

career prospects had made her feel dangerously alone. It wasn't just herself she needed to support—Nicky was counting on her, too.

She fastened up his tiny dungarees and let him squirm off the mat and crawl away. She and Vasco both watched him scoot out of the dining room and back into the kitchen.

"Wassat?" A delighted cry accompanied by rustling alerted them that he'd discovered the wrapped gifts Vasco brought.

"Is he allowed to open them?"

"That's what they're for." They followed him into the kitchen where he'd already pulled the shiny silver paper off a large box containing a Thomas the Tank Engine starter set that must have cost almost as much as her book. Nicky put the corner of the box in his mouth.

Vasco laughed. "I bought the most delicious train I could find."

"He'll love it." She pulled the box out of Nicky's arms. "Let me open it up, sweetie."

Nicky reached for the next gift, a sparkly blue one.

Vasco shrugged. "I missed his first birthday." He watched with joy in his eyes as Nicky skinned the present, an elaborate construction set made from pieces of carved wood.

"You're good at picking age-appropriate stuff." She was relieved nothing so far looked like a choking hazard.

"I'm good at asking for and taking expert advice." His eyes met hers, and an annoying shiver sizzled down her spine. Again his voice had been almost suggestive.

Shame her body was so keen to pick up on the suggestion.

He'd removed his jacket, and she was chagrined to discover that his jeans hugged his well-formed backside in an appetizing way. Unfortunately, every time she looked at him something inside her lit up like Christmas tree lights, which was not at all appropriate to the situation.

Maybe Karen was right and she needed a little romance—or at least sex—in her life. Just to take the edge off, or something.

But not with Vasco. Since he was the father of her child, that would be way too heavy. And it was unlikely that a dashing royal bachelor would be interested in a short, frumpy book restorer. He probably looked at everyone like that.

The third gift, wrapped in green shimmery paper, proved to be a stuffed purple dinosaur. Not one with its own PBS show, happily, but rather an expensive, handmade-looking one with plush fur. "I don't know what kind of toys he likes, so I got a mix."

"Very sensible." She pulled apart the stiff plastic of the train packaging and set some cars down on the floor. Nicky spun them across the polished wood with a whoop of glee. "That one's a hit."

Vasco assembled the track, complete with bridges and a tunnel and two junctions, and helped Nicky get the train going around it.

Stella watched with a mix of quiet joy and stone-cold terror. Nicky was already getting attached to Vasco. She could see from the look of curiosity in his big, gray eyes that he liked the large new man in his kitchen. So far Vasco seemed to be thoughtful and kind. She'd worried about Nicky not having a father in his life, particularly if he needed male guidance as he got older.

Vasco's appearance seemed to offer a lot of exciting possibilities for him. And some rather worrying ones, too. Was Nicky expected to be king of Montmajor someday?

She'd better confirm that Vasco was Nicky's biological father before this situation went any further. "I need to take Nicky out and run some errands. How about we stop by the lab on the way and drop off the DNA samples."

Would he go there with her? That way she'd know he was serious, and wasn't going to pay someone off to produce the results he wanted.

He stood up and his dark brows lowered over narrowed eyes. For a moment she thought he'd say no or find an excuse. Doubts sprang to her mind—who was this man she'd allowed to play on the floor with her son, who she'd promised to move in with for a full month?

Then he nodded. "Sure. Let's go."

The DNA test results which arrived three days later confirmed what Vasco knew in his heart from the moment he saw Nicky—the boy was his flesh and blood.

He arrived on their doorstep that afternoon laden with more packages. Not the silly toys he'd brought last time, but luggage for their journey. He knew Stella was strapped for cash and it was easier to give her things than offer her money. She'd already turned that down when he'd offered at their last meeting.

He hadn't bothered to phone ahead, so she was surprised, and answered the door in a rather fetching pair of bike shorts and a tank top. She gasped when she saw him. "I was working out." She looked like she wanted to cover herself with her hands. "Pilates." She blushed.

"No wonder you look so good." Her body was delicious. Fit without being too slim, with high, plump breasts that beckoned his palms to cup them.

Lucky thing his palms were wrapped around suitcase handles. "I bought some bags for the trip and printed copies of your eTickets. I'll come by to pick you up when we leave for the airport."

Stella's pink mouth formed a round O.

"You did say you could leave anytime after Wednesday, so I booked us on a flight for Thursday. Plenty of time to pack."

"Did you book the return trip?" Her voice sounded a bit strained.

"Not yet, since we don't know how long you'll be staying." He smiled, in a way that he hoped was reassuring. He did not intend for them to come back, but it was far too early for her to know that. "Where shall I put these?"

Her eyes widened further at the sight of the luggage in his hands. "I didn't know Coach made suitcases."

"They're good quality." He decided to walk in and put them down. Maybe she was a little flustered by her Pilates workout. "Where's Nicky?"

"Napping."

"He naps a lot."

"They do at this age, which is a blessing since it's the only way I can do anything for myself. I can't take my eyes off him for an instant lately before he's climbing onto the back of the sofa or tugging on the lamp cords."

"In Montmajor you'll have plenty of time to yourself.

All the ladies in the palace are fighting with each other for the chance to take care of him."

"Ladies?" Her face paled.

"Older ladies with gray hair." He fought the urge to chuckle. Had she seen them as competition? "They won't try to take him away from you, just to squeeze his cheeks a lot and cluck over him."

She blew out a breath. "It's a lot to take in. Nicky has the advantage of being too young to worry about everything."

He wanted to take her in his arms and give her a reassuring hug, but right now he could see that would be anything but reassuring. Her whole body stiffened up whenever he came within about five feet of her.

There'd be plenty of time for caressing and soothing once they arrived in Montmajor. "Don't you worry about anything. I'll take great care of both of you."

Four

The journey to Montmajor was an adventure in itself. Naturally everyone assumed they were a family. Stella was called Mrs. Montoya twice at the airport, even though her ticket and passport were in her own name.

Vasco carried Nicky at every opportunity, and the little boy looked quite at home in his strong arms. Vasco himself beamed with paternal pride, and handled each situation from Stella's overweight luggage to Nicky running around the airport—he'd started walking that Monday, and quickly progressed to sprinting—with good humor and tireless charm.

And then there were the stares.

Every woman in the airport, from the headphone-wearing teenagers to the elderly bathroom attendants, stared at Vasco wherever he went. His easy swagger and piratical good looks drew female attention like a beacon. He wore a long, dark raincoat—it was pouring when they left—and army green pants with black boots, so no one would have guessed he was a king. His passport was black and larger than hers, bearing an elaborate seal, and she wondered if all his royal titles were listed inside.

He still had to go through security like everyone else, but he'd bought them some kind of VIP tickets that entitled them to fly past most of the lines and get right onto the plane with almost no waiting.

Stella tried to ignore the envious looks. She certainly didn't feel smug about strolling around with Vasco. Probably none of these people would covet the situation she was in, her future uncertain and her son's affections at stake.

The long plane ride passed quickly. Nicky sat between them in the wide first-class seats, and they were both so busy keeping him entertained, or being agonizingly quiet while he napped, that she didn't have to worry about keeping a conversation going.

A small private plane met them at Barcelona Airport for the rest of the journey to Montmajor, whose airport wasn't large enough for commercial jets.

Suddenly things felt different. Men in black jackets with walkie-talkies swept them onto the plane, bowing to Vasco and generally treating him like a monarch. The inside of the plane was arranged like a lounge, with plush purple leather seats and a well-stocked bar. Except for takeoff and landing, Nicky was allowed the run of the plane, and two stern male attendants indulged his every whim. Vasco smiled and watched.

Stella felt herself shrinking into the background. They were now in Vasco's world and she wasn't at all sure of her place there.

Once they'd landed, a black limo drove them from the airport through some hilly countryside, then up toward an imposing sandstone castle with a wide, arched entrance. Inside the arch, the castle spread out around them, long galleries of carved stone columns lining a paved courtyard.

People rushed out from all directions to greet them. Vasco put his arm around her and introduced her— in Catalan she presumed, since it sounded somewhere between Spanish and French—with a proprietary air that made her stomach flip.

Did he want people to think they were a couple? His arm around her shoulders set alarm bells ringing all over her body. She gripped Nicky's hand with force. She hadn't got used to him toddling beside her rather than traveling in her arms.

"Stella, this is my aunt Frida, my aunt Mari and my aunt Lilli." Three women, all dressed in black and too old to be literally his aunts, nodded and smiled and gazed longingly at Nicky. She'd presumed that his father was dead, or he wouldn't be king, but it hadn't occurred to her to ask about his mother or any siblings. How blindly she'd walked into this whole thing.

"Nice to meet you," she stammered. They didn't extend their hands to shake, which was lucky as she didn't want to let go of Nicky. He seemed the safest anchor in this strange, foreign world. Vasco's arm still rested on her neck, his fingers curling gently around her shoulder.

"I'll take Stella inside and show her around." He squeezed her shoulder with his fingers, which made her eyes widen, then ushered her up a wide flight of stairs and through a double door into a large foyer. A vast woven tapestry covered one stone wall—a hunting scene, lavishly decorated with foliage and flowers. Vasco walked toward a curving flight of stone stairs with a carved balustrade. "And on the way we'll pass by the library, which I suspect is far more interesting to you than your bedroom."

Another squeeze made her heart beat faster. He seemed to be giving the false impression that they were involved. Her face heated and she wondered how she could pull away without seeming rude. Anger rose inside her alongside the heat Vasco seemed to generate whenever he came near her. It wasn't fair of him to toy with her like this. She bent down, pretending to adjust Nicky's dungarees, and managed to slip from his grasp.

Vasco simply strode ahead, pointing out what lay behind each carved doorway. An attendant had taken his raincoat so she had an annoying view of his tight rear end as he marched along the hallway. She tugged her eyes to the timeworn stone carvings that lined the walls.

Nicky pulled his grip from hers and ran forward, toward Vasco. A shriek of glee bounced off the ancient stone and echoed around them. Vasco turned to her with a grin on his face. "Just what this old place needs— some youthful enthusiasm." She couldn't help smiling.

The library was every bit as awe-inspiring as she could have dreamed. Two stories of volumes lined its walls and the long oak table in the center of the room was scarred by centuries of scholars and their ink. Nicky ran up to an ancient chair and she dashed to scoop him up before he could pull it over on himself. She couldn't even begin to imagine what treasures must lurk on those high shelves, accessed by rolling ladders.

The one tall window was shaded, probably to protect the books from sun, so the room had a mystical gloom that fueled her excitement.

Nicky yawned and fidgeted, and for a second she felt guilty about wanting to be alone with all those magnificent books. "He needs a nap."

"Or a good run." Vasco took Nicky's other hand. "Come on, Nicky!" He took off toward the door, with Nicky running beside him. Stella stood staring after her son for a moment, then hurried after them, torn between her pleasure at watching Nicky so secure on his tiny feet, and fearing that the pace of everything, including her son's development, was happening way too fast for her to keep up.

With Nicky tucked up in bed, under the watchful eye of one of the "aunts," Stella joined Vasco in the grand dining room for supper. The majestic surroundings demanded elegant attire, and in anticipation she'd made sure to bring several dresses with her. Karen was a talented thrift shop hunter and had scored four lovely vintage dresses for her at her favorite shop in an expensive neighborhood, each from a different era. Tonight she wore a rather fitted 1950s dress in steel-gray silk. Its perfect condition suggested that it had never been worn, and the crisp fabric hugged her body like reassuring armor. Karen loved to choose matching accessories, so tiny clusters of 1950s paste diamonds ornamented her ears. She had one pair of shoes for all her ensembles, gunmetal silver with pointed toes and medium heels. She tucked her hair into a 1950s-style chignon and felt—if not as glamorous as the type of women Vasco was used to—pretty elegant and well put together.

Vasco rose from the table as she descended a small flight of stairs into the dining room. His gray eyes swept her from head to toe, and darkened with appreciation. He walked toward her, took her hand and kissed it.

"You look stunning." Throaty and sincere, his words made her blink.

Luckily the stiff peaks of silk hid the way her nipples tightened under his admiring gaze. "Thanks. Jeans and a T-shirt didn't feel right for dinner in such a dramatic environment."

Vasco himself wore tailored black pants and a fine-striped shirt, open at the collar. Considerably more formal than his clothes in the U.S. "I'm not sure it matters what you wear here. The palace drapes around one like a velvet robe." His white teeth flashed a grin. "But you make everything around you vanish."

Her hand tingled where his lips had touched it. Normally this kind of flattery would make her roll her eyes, but from Vasco's lips it sounded oddly sincere. He pulled out a carved chair and she sat in it. The table was elaborately set for the two of them. Glass goblets glittered with both red and white wine, and the silver cutlery shone from recent polishing. As soon as Vasco was seated, two waiters appeared carrying an array of dishes, which they offered to her one by one, spooning their contents onto her plate when she agreed.

She didn't understand the words they'd said but the aromas spoke for themselves. Crispy-skinned game hen, fragrant rice with snippets of fresh herbs and a rich ratatouille. Her mouth watered.

"It's good to be home." Vasco smiled at the feast. "I

miss the cooking almost more than anything when I'm gone."

"How long were you gone? When you were younger, I mean." She wanted to know more about his past, and the circumstances that had conspired to bring them together.

"Almost ten years." He took a swig of red wine. "I left when I was eighteen and I didn't plan to ever come back."

"Why not?" He seemed so deeply rooted in the place.

"There's only room for one male heir in Montmajor. He inherits the palace, the crown, the country and everything in it. Any other male heirs must set forth to seek their fortune elsewhere. It's a thousand-year-old tradition."

"But why?"

"To avoid conflict and struggles for the throne. One of my ancestors made it a law after he seized the throne from his own older brother. On his eighteenth birthday the younger son must leave the country with a thousand Quirils in his pocket. It's been enforced rigidly ever since."

"So they literally drove you out of the country on your eighteenth birthday."

"No one had to drive me. I knew to make myself scarce."

Stella tried not to shiver. She couldn't imagine what it would feel like growing up knowing you'd be banished one day. "And I bet one thousand Quirils doesn't go as far as it did a thousand years ago."

Vasco laughed. "Nope. Then it was the equivalent of a couple of million dollars. Now it's about seventy-five."

"What did your parents think of all this?"

He shrugged. "It's the law." The candlelight emphasized the strong planes of his face. "I suppose I thought they wouldn't enforce it. What boy thinks his own parents plan to send him away? But when the time drew near…and there was my brother." Vasco's brow lowered and his whole expression seemed to darken.

Stella gulped down a morsel of tender meat. She had the feeling she'd hit on a very sensitive topic. "I assume your brother is dead." She said it as quietly as possible. "Which is why you came home."

"Yes. He killed himself and both my parents in a car accident. Drunk at the time, as usual." He growled the words. "And it's over all of their dead bodies that I'm back here." His eyes flashed, and he took another swig of wine. "Lovely story, isn't it?"

She drew in a breath. "I'm so sorry."

"That was nine months ago, when my father's oldest friend called me up and told me to return." He raised a brow. "I flew back the following day for the first time in ten years."

Something in his expression touched her. He looked wistful. "You must have missed Montmajor while you were away."

"Like a missing part of me." His gray eyes were serious. "I didn't think I'd ever see it again."

"The laws demanded that you never even visit?"

He nodded. "In case I was tempted to lead a coup." His eyes sparkled with humor. "Paranoid country, huh?"

"Very." Stella swallowed some wine. Was Nicky heir to the throne here? The question seemed far too huge to just say out loud. "Do you plan to change the law, so that if you have several children the younger ones don't have to be turfed out at age 18?"

"Already did it." He grinned. "My first edict when I came back. People were really happy about it. That and I made it legal to have sex outside marriage."

Stella laughed. "I bet that law was broken a lot anyway."

"I know it. Sounded pretty funny when the official speaker pronounced it from the castle walls. Maybe that's why no one ever had the nerve to change it before."

"So I guess you're not under pressure to marry anyone in order to enjoy life."

"That's a fact." He smiled and lifted his glass. "Marriage and the Montoya men generally don't agree with each other."

Stella lifted her glass, but wondered what he meant. Did he not intend to marry? If Nicky was his heir he didn't need to. The next in line was already born and he hadn't had to break any ancient laws, either. "Maybe you just haven't met the right person yet."

Vasco's eyes darkened. "Or maybe I have?"

His suggestive tone sent a ripple of awareness to her core, and she shifted slightly in her fitted dress. "There must be a lot of women who'd be happy to be your queen."

"Oh yes. They've been coming out of the woodwork from all over." His dimples showed. "A crown has amazing aphrodisiac effects."

Not that he needed them. With those looks he wasn't in much danger of being lonely. But could he marry some glamorous woman and expect that she'd put up with his sperm bank son becoming king?

Frightening as it was, she needed a clearer picture of what he had in mind. "What are you hoping for, with Nicky? He's not really next in line to the throne, is he?" The whole thing sounded so ridiculous that she blushed when she said it. Maybe a lot of moms would love their child to carry a scepter, but she wasn't one of them.

"Right now he is. He's my only heir." Vasco frowned. "However, if I were to marry someone, the first son I had with her would become heir. Children born in marriage take precedence over illegitimate heirs."

"That doesn't seem fair." Indignation flared in her chest, which was insane, considering that she didn't want Nicky to be king. Still, it implied that somehow he was less important, and maybe that tugged at her sense of guilt over choosing to bring him into the world in a nontraditional family.

"You're right. It's not. I could change the law but it doesn't seem to be an urgent problem right now."

"Not like the need to have unmarried sex."

"Exactly." His eyes twinkled. "First things first."

Heat sizzled inside her and she wished his seductive gaze didn't have such a dramatic effect. She had no intention of having any kind of sex with him. She'd managed without sex for more than two years since she broke up with Trevor, and hadn't missed it at all. Of course being woken up several times a night by a baby could put a damper on anyone's libido. Maybe now that she was getting sleep again it had come back?

Not a very convenient time for lust to reappear in her life. She tugged her gaze to her plate and pushed some rice onto her fork.

"How did you get into restoring books?"

The innocuous question surprised her. What a change

of subject. "It happened by accident. My mom had an old edition of *Alice in Wonderland* that had belonged to her great-grandmother, and she gave it to me when I was in college. The spine was starting to come apart so I asked for advice at a local bookseller, who told me about a course in book restoring—and I got hooked. There's something addictive about restoring someone's treasure so it can be enjoyed by another generation of readers."

"An appreciation for the past is one thing that links us. My ancestors have lived here for more than a millennium and I grew up walking in their footsteps, using their furnishings and reading their books." He gestured at the long wood table, its surface polished to a sheen but scarred with tiny nicks by generations of diners.

"It must be nice to have such a sense of belonging."

"It is, until you're turned out of the place where you belong." He lifted a brow. "Then you search and search for somewhere else to belong."

"Did you find that place?"

He laughed. "Never. Not until I came home. Though I traveled far and wide looking for it." His expression turned serious. "I want Nicky to have that sense of belonging. To grow up breathing the air of his ancestral homeland, singing our songs and eating our food."

Stella swallowed. He was getting carried away and she'd better set some boundaries right now. "I can understand why you feel that way, but you didn't write any of that…" She leaned in and whispered. "In the sperm donor information." She put down her fork. "Because if you had I wouldn't have chosen you as the donor. You gave away the right to decide what happens to Nicky when you visited Westlake Cryobank."

His eyes narrowed. "I made a terrible mistake."

"We all have to live with our mistakes." She could say she'd made one in choosing Vasco as Nicky's father—except that now she had Nicky, the center of her world. "Don't think you can tell me and Nicky what to do." She tried to sound stern. "Just because you're a king and from a thousand-year-old dynasty…" she gestured around the elegant chamber "…doesn't mean that you're more important or special than me and Nicky or that your needs and desires come first. We were raised in American democracy where everyone is equal—at least in theory—and I intend to keep it that way."

Humor flashed in his eyes. "I like your fire. I'd never coerce you into staying. After a few days or weeks in Montmajor I doubt you'll be able to imagine living anywhere else."

"We'll see about that." Soft golden candlelight reflected in the polished glass of their goblets and illuminated the ancient sandstone walls around them. Already Montmajor was beginning its process of seduction.

And so was Vasco.

He tilted his head, smiling at her. "Let's take a walk before dessert." He rose and rounded the table, then extended his hand.

She cursed the way her fingers tingled as she slid them inside his. Still, she rose to her feet and followed him, heels clicking on the stone floor as she walked with him through a vast wooden double door into a tall gallery and out onto a veranda.

They stood high above the surrounding landscape.

The last sliver of sun was setting in the west—to their left—and the mountains fell away at their feet like crumpled tissue paper. As the peaks disappeared into the mist she almost thought she could make out the shimmering glass of the Mediterranean sea in the far distance.

Hardly any sign of human habitation was visible. Just the odd clay-tiled roof of a remote homestead, or the winding ribbon of a distant road. "Amazing," she managed when she caught her breath. "I bet it looked like this in medieval times."

"In medieval times there were more people." Vasco smiled, the sun highlighting his bronzed features and deepening the laugh lines around his eyes. "This area was a center for weaving and leatherwork. Our population is about half what it was in the tenth century. We're one of Europe's best kept secrets and I think most people here like it that way."

His thumb stroked the outside of her hand and sent heat slithering up it. Again her nipples tightened inside her gray silk dress and she sucked in a breath and pulled her hand back. "What about schools? How are the children educated?" Anything to get the conversation on some kind of prosaic track, so she wasn't falling prey to the seductive majesty of the landscape and its monarch.

"There's only one school, in the town. It's one of the finest educational institutions in Europe. Children here learn all the major European languages—now Chinese is popular, too—and go on to university at places like Harvard and Cambridge, the University of Barcelona. All over the world."

"Don't you lose a lot of well-educated people that way? When they go on to work in other countries."

"Sure, for a while. But they always come back." He gestured at the dramatic landscape around them. "Where else can you live once you've left your heart in Montmajor?"

Stella felt an odd flutter in her chest. The place was already taking hold of her. "I'd like to see the town." She glanced at him. "There is a town, isn't there?"

"We call it the city." His white teeth flashed in the setting sun. "And it would be my great pleasure to give you a tour tomorrow. Let's go finish dinner."

She stiffened as he slid his arm inside hers. Really, she should protest at all these intimate gestures, but somehow that felt petty, when he might just think he was being a gracious host. People were different in this part of the world, more demonstrative and touchy-feely, and she didn't want to come across like an uptight puritan when she'd chosen for her son to have Mediterranean heritage.

Her own elbow jostled against his soft shirt, and the hairs on her arm stood on end. In fact every inch of her body stood to attention as they strolled through a dimly illuminated forest of stone columns back to the candlelit dining room.

Their plates had been cleared and as soon as they sat—Vasco pulled out her chair, old-world style— servants appeared with gleaming platters of glazed pears and homemade ice cream.

Stella's eyes widened. "I'm not going to fit into any of my clothes after a week here."

"That would be a shame." Vasco glanced up, mischief dancing in his eyes. "That dress fits you so beautifully." His gaze flicked to her chest, which jumped in excitement.

She felt heat rising to her face. "I'll have to do some exercise."

"There's nowhere better. Tomorrow we can ride in the hills."

"On a horse? I've never ridden in my life."

"You could learn. Or we could walk."

"I like the second option. Nicky can't walk too far, though. He's only starting."

"Nicky can stay with his new aunts while you and I stride through the landscape."

She had to admit that sounded pretty good. "I used to walk in the hills all the time, but since I had Nicky it's been hard to find the time."

"Here we'll have all the time in the world." His smile broadened. "And we can do *anything* you like."

The emphasis sent a shiver down her spine. Already her body had a few suggestions, mostly involving peeling those well-cut clothes off Vasco's ripped and tanned physique.

What was it about this guy that set her on fire? Maybe his being Nicky's father had something to do with it. There was already a bond between them, forged in blood, a connection with him that went far beyond their brief acquaintance.

And maybe the strange and worrying situation had set her nerves on edge, which made her emotions and senses all the more likely to flare up in unexpected ways. She'd have to watch out for that.

"When you look out the window tomorrow and see the sunrise, you'll know you've come home." Vasco's voice startled her out of her thoughts. His eyes heavy-lidded, he looked at her over a sparkling glass of white wine.

"I'm not at all sure I'll be awake at sunrise."

"I could come rouse you." His eyes glittered.

"No, thanks!" She said it too fast, and a little too loud. She needed to keep this man out of her bedroom.

Which might be a very serious challenge.

Five

Stella had rather dreaded seeing Vasco's handsome countenance over the breakfast table the next morning, but found herself put out when he wasn't here. Apparently he'd gone off on royal business and wouldn't be back until late. So much for her tour of the town and walk in the hills.

Was she turning into a pouting, jealous girlfriend, when she wasn't even his girlfriend?

"Ma!" Nicky played with the omelet the kitchen staff had made for him. "Cheerios!"

"Hey, you can say real words when you truly need something." She wiped his chin. "But I'm not sure they have Cheerios here."

"Cheerios!" He banged his spoon on the gleaming wood surface of the table, which made Stella seize his wrist and glance over her shoulder to see if anyone else had witnessed the desecration.

"This table is very precious, sweetie. We have to be careful with it."

"Cheerios, peez." His big gray eyes now brimmed with tears. Why hadn't she thought to bring some with her? She'd had a ziplock bag of them for the plane, but she hadn't thought about people eating different foods here.

"I'll go ask the cook, okay? We'll find something."

She left him at the table and pushed open the door that the staff seemed to appear and disappear from. She was a little alarmed to find a young man hovering right behind it. "Do you have any breakfast cereal?" She spoke in Spanish. He nodded and summoned her into a tiled hallway that led to a series of pantries. One of them turned out to be lined floor to ceiling with boxes of pasta, crackers and cereals, all imported from the U.S.

"For little Nicky," he said with a smile. "His Majesty requested them."

Stella bit her lip. How thoughtful. She pointed at the giant box of Cheerios on a high shelf. "Could he have some of those in a bowl—no milk?"

"Of course, Madam."

She heaved a sigh of relief—or was it awe—and walked back to the table. Alarm filled her heart when she pushed through the door and saw Nicky's chair empty. He always sat in a high chair at home but they didn't seem to have one here.

"Nicky?" She glanced around the room. There was no sign of him. And so many doors he could have gone out through. Panic snapped through her. This palace was vast, and probably had plenty of high walls and ledges a child could fall off. It wasn't safe to leave him unattended for a single moment in such a labyrinthine and nonchildproof space, and she'd have to keep that in mind from now on. "Nicky?"

She hurried out into the main hallway, and waved to an older footman. "Excuse me, I… My son…"

He simply smiled and gestured for her to follow him. More doors and stone hallways—they all looked alike, even though they weren't—led to an interior courtyard with a large, round pool in the middle. A fountain bubbled water and her pulse began to return to normal when she saw Nicky floating a small wooden sailboat in the water under the watchful gaze of two of the "aunts."

She heaved a sigh. "Thank goodness you're here! Sweetie, please don't take off without telling me where you're going." As if he could have explained it. Still, she wanted the women to know, since they must have brought him here. "Mommy needs to know where you are at all times."

She gave the "aunts" a frosty smile. "This water looks rather deep." She spoke in Spanish. They gave no sign of having understood. The fountain was lovely, but the patterned tiles at the bottom of the pool shimmered beneath a good foot and a half of water. Quite enough for a toddler to drown in if someone's back was turned. She'd have to talk to Vasco about safety, so he could lay down some guidelines for the "aunts."

"I found you some Cheerios, Nicky. Come have some." She held out her hand. He glanced up at her, then turned his attention right back to the sailboat. It was quite an elaborate one with cotton rigging and a striped sail. "We'll come back to the boat after breakfast."

"No! Nicky sail boat."

Her eyes widened at the longest sentence he'd ever said. "Have some Cheerios first." Her eyes turned to the aunts in a silent plea.

"Don't worry, Ms. Greco. He just ate two cherry pastries." The smaller aunt—Mari—spoke in flawless, barely accented English. "And we'll take care of him while you eat your own breakfast and do anything else you like."

Cherry pastries? Not the most nutritious breakfast, but at least he'd eaten. And maybe she could go have hers quickly. "Are you sure?"

"I raised eight of my own children and there's nothing I'd like better than to spend time with little Nicky. Frida feels the same and when Lilli's back from her doctor's appointment, she'd agree, too." She beamed at Nicky. "He's such a dear child."

"Yes." Stella bit her lip. "You won't let him fall into the water." It was a statement not a question.

"Absolutely not." Frida's reply showed that she spoke perfect English, too. Stella felt embarrassed for thinking they wouldn't. Though Mari was already speaking softly to Nicky in Catalan, encouraging him to move one of the sails, from what she could gather. "Vasco tells us you restore antique books. We're so lucky to enjoy your expertise here. I used to be a professor of medieval literature at the University of Barcelona, and I know this palace is a treasure trove."

Stella swallowed. "Yes. I saw some of the library yesterday. Maybe I will go there now. We'll have to have a long chat later." She was far too flustered to talk now. These white-haired old grannies were more accomplished and educated than she'd ever be.

Never mind what they could teach her son—*she* could probably learn a lot from them. "I'll see you later."

She kissed Nicky on the forehead, trying to ignore her maternal misgivings at leaving him in such capable hands. No worse than leaving him at the local day care, which she'd used regularly for work.

She spent the day in the library fondling impressive volumes dating back to the time of Charlemagne. Vasco had arranged for a selection of the finest restoration tools, including a vast array of delicate leathers and sheets of gold leaf, to be used for repairing or replacing damaged covers.

Just touching the books was a sensual experience. Reading the words, stories, poems and dramatic tales from history brought her imagination to life. She knew French and Spanish, and quite a bit of Latin and Italian, so she could understand and enjoy much of what she read in the same way the lucky residents of this palace must have done for generations.

She made mental notes of different things she wanted to show Vasco, because she thought he'd enjoy them: tales from his own family history, intriguing Montmajor folktales, even a journal of sorts written by a young king in the 1470s.

But Vasco didn't show up that afternoon.

He was absent at dinnertime, which made her feel rather silly in the aqua vintage maxi dress Karen had chosen for her along with some pretty turquoise earrings. She ate alone in the grand dining room, wishing she'd shared Nicky's feast of scrambled eggs and toast. Nicky was now tucked up in bed under the watchful gaze of a local girl. It was awkward sitting there as waiters brought dishes to her and refilled her glass, and she stared at the empty chair on the other side of the table.

Where was Vasco? Of course it wasn't really her business. They weren't involved or anything. Even if he was out to dinner with another woman, that was absolutely fine.

She swallowed more wine. Maybe she wasn't so crazy about the idea of him carrying on with other women while she and Nicky were there. Couldn't he save that for after they'd gone? They were his guests, after all.

He was probably at a party, schmoozing with wealthy aristocrats, and had forgotten all about them. Or maybe he'd flown off somewhere in his purple-seated plane, to spend a few days on someone's yacht or attend a grand wedding.

Why did she care? She was busy and happy with the library and its amazing collection of books and manuscripts. So why did she glance up and catch her breath every time the door opened? And why did her heart sink each time she saw it was just the waiter again?

She only ate half of the pretty apricot tart in its lake of fresh cream. It seemed a shame to waste such carefully prepared and delicious food, but then it was also foolish to eat it if she wasn't hungry and no one was here to share the pleasure.

She'd removed her napkin from her lap and was about to head upstairs to her room, when the door opened again. This time her startled glance and increased pulse rate were rewarded by the appearance of the man whose presence seemed to hover everywhere in the palace.

Gray eyes flashing, and hair tousled by the wind,

Vasco swept into the room like a sirocco. "I'm so sorry I missed dinner."

He strode toward her, long legs clad in dusty black pants. A white T-shirt clung to his pecs and biceps, revealing a physique more developed and chiseled than her wildest imaginings.

She struggled to find a sensible thing to say, and failed. "Where have you been?"

He looked surprised, and she regretted her rude question. "I rode over to Monteleon, to visit an old friend. We got to talking and the hours slipped away."

So that was the "royal business" he'd been called away on? Again she felt slightly offended. She wondered if the old friend was male or female, but she didn't want to know that. "I found some interesting things in the library."

"Oh?" He'd rounded the table, where he picked up her wineglass and drank from it. Before she had time to blink, a rather flustered male waiter appeared with a filled glass for him. He thanked the waiter, but as soon as the man had disappeared he looked ruefully at his glass. "I'm sure this won't taste as good as one blessed by your lips."

Then he sipped and walked on around the table, leaving Stella staring after him. How did he get away with saying stuff like that? She glanced at her own glass back on the table, and it suddenly seemed unbearably sensual to drink from it again.

"I thought I should start the restoration project by focusing on books and papers that directly relate to the royal family. I've found quite a few interesting things buried amongst the other books, and I thought you might want to organize them into a separate archive of their own."

"Great idea." He was now at the far end of the table, where he put his glass down and stretched, which sent ripples traveling through the muscles of his broad back.

Was he trying to taunt her with his impressive physique? He should know by now that she was the bookish type and didn't notice such things. "Would you like me to show you the book I plan to work on first? After you have dinner, of course."

"I've had dinner." His eyes wandered to her cleavage, which swelled under his admiring gaze. "Though I wish I'd had it here instead. The view is much better." His gaze drifted lower, which made her belly tighten, then to her hips, which had to resist a powerful urge to sway under his intense stare.

"It was strange eating all alone in this big dining room."

"I apologize for making you do that. I'll make sure it never happens again."

She didn't quite believe him. He was a flatterer who knew the right thing to say at any moment. Like his promise of taking her for a walk today.

"Shall we head to the library now?"

"Sure." He walked back to her and slid his arm around her waist. Her eyes opened wide as a shiver of sheer arousal snapped through her. How many glasses of wine had she drunk? Surely it was only two, though it was hard to keep track when they kept refilling it for her.

"I am dusty. Maybe we should stop by my room on the way so I can change. No need to add any dust to the considerable amount that must be on the books already."

His smile made her knees weak. She cursed herself for it. "No need. Did you ride your horse there?"

"Many horses." He grinned. "My bike. It's a far better way to get around these mountains than a big royal sedan. The dirt is the only drawback. I should have showered before coming to find you, but I couldn't wait."

Her cheeks heated under his glance, and she sucked in a breath. Her pewter shoes made an impressive noise on the stone flags of the grand hallway. Vasco turned to the right, in a direction she'd never been before. The carvings on the walls grew more elaborate and the floor turned into an intricate mosaic, which led to a grand, arched doorway.

"The royal bedchamber?" She looked up at the embossed shield carved right into the stone above the door.

"Exactly." He made a courtly gesture with his hand. "Please come in."

She didn't have much choice with his arm still tucked around her waist. A vast bed rose almost to the twenty-foot high ceiling. Heavy curtains hung from a carved wood frame. Candles burned in elaborate candelabra on each side of the room, throwing off a surprising amount of light.

"They've invented something called electricity. Have you heard of it?" The host of candles made shapes and colors dance on the walls and ceiling.

"These newfangled inventions never last. Much better to stick with what's tried and true." She saw his dimples for a second before he peeled off his white T-shirt to reveal bronzed muscles that made her jaw drop.

When he unbuttoned his pants she turned away. "Maybe I should wait outside?"

"No need. I'll be ready in a moment."

He was doing this to torment her. And it was working. She couldn't resist sneaking a peak in the age-clouded mirror than hung on a nearby wall. His tight backside looked very fetching in classic white underwear. His thighs were powerful and dusted with dark hair, and she admired them for a split second before they disappeared into a crisply ironed pair of black pants that seemed to have appeared out of thin air.

He stretched again, causing her to close her eyes for a moment. No one needed that much overstimulation. When she opened them she was relieved to see his thick biceps hidden behind the creamy cotton of a collarless shirt.

"Now I'm ready. Take me to your library." He walked toward her, barefoot on the stone floor, a smile in his gray eyes.

Stella swallowed. Her library? Obviously he'd decided it was her domain for the duration of her stay, which gave her an interesting feeling of pleasure.

Vasco took her cold, rather nervous hand in his warm one, and they set off along the corridor. Even with her in heels and him barefoot she only came up to his cheekbone—and a dramatic, well-shaped cheekbone it was.

Anticipation tingled through her veins as she switched on the low hanging lights in the library, illuminating the magical kingdom of books. She led him to the table where she'd started to arrange the volumes most in need of repair. One heavy tome, its delicate leather cover almost in tatters, sat apart from the others.

Vasco ran his fingers over the rough surface, where the tooled gold had all but vanished under the wear of centuries of hands. "It's a history of Montmajor."

"Written in 1370." Stella laughed. "Rather amazing that they had so much to write already."

"We always have a lot to say about ourselves." That mischievous white grin flashed in his tanned face. "And apparently we love to read about ourselves, too."

He flipped open the book with a casual hand, which almost made Stella want to grab his wrist. This book was six hundred and fifty years old, after all. Vasco began to read, his deep, rich voice wrapping itself around the handwritten Catalan words that she could almost understand, but not quite. Something swelled inside her as Vasco spoke the ancient words aloud with obvious enjoyment.

He stopped and looked at her. "Do you know what it says?"

"I need to learn Catalan. I know French and Spanish and a little Italian and it sounds to me like it's a bit of all of them mixed together."

"It's so much more than that." His eyes narrowed into a smile. "I'll have to teach you."

"That's a big project."

"Then we'll tackle it one word at a time." He pressed a finger to his sensual mouth. "First things first. What's the most important thing in life?"

Stella frowned. "Good health?"

Vasco shook his head. "Passion. *La passio.*"

"La passio." She let the word roll off her tongue, and decided not to start a debate about how crucial passion was to people who were starving. Kings clearly lived in a rather more gilded and hedonistic reality.

"Ben fet."

"I'm guessing that means *well done,* since it sounds a bit like *bien fait* in French."

His grin widened. "You're catching on. Soon you'll be speaking it like a native."

She couldn't help a little flush of pride. "I'll do my best. I can't help but feel *la passio* for the work I'll be doing." She glanced down at the lovely book and managed to restrain herself from moving Vasco's large hand from the page. No need to bore him with her worries about natural oils seeping into ancient handmade paper and tiny microscopic creatures eating away at natural inks. "I plan to restore the cover first. I'll preserve the original then make a leather slipcover that mirrors how it would have looked when new. Then I'll go through page by page and stabilize the book. The inside is in surprisingly good shape."

"Which means it hasn't been read enough times, yet." He flipped a page and started to read again, letting his tongue wrap around the words, bringing them to life in the quiet library.

Stella watched, entranced. Even though the book was about history, it was written in some kind of verse, and Vasco's voice rode the cadence of the words in a sensual rhythm. She could figure out the meaning of enough words to recognize a description of a battle, lances flying and flags fluttering in the wind, horses galloping on an open plain. The vision of it all danced before her eyes, brought to life centuries after it was written so painstakingly in the book.

Her heart was beating fast by the time Vasco stopped, or pulled up, since it felt more as if she'd been riding

along in the tale and they'd slid to a halt, dust flying
and hooves clattering.

"Beautiful." Her voice was breathless, as if she'd
been running alongside the riders.

"Bell." Vasco smiled. "And thank you for awakening
me to it. I'd never have opened this book if you weren't
here. I confess I'm not much of a reader, by nature."

"You're more action oriented." She noticed how
Vasco always seemed to have the wind in his hair, even
here in the quiet calm of the library. "And this book has
a lot of action in it."

"It does. And plenty of *passio.*" He took her hand
in his. Part of her was glad he'd removed it from the
fragile old book, but the rest of her started to quiver in
a mix of excitement and terror as desire rose inside her,
hot and inevitable.

Was this just a friendly gesture for him? Everything
about Vasco was sensual and dramatic, so maybe she
read too much into his bold touches and looks. Her hand
heated inside his and her fingers tingled with the desire
to explore his warm skin. All the sexual feelings that
had lain dormant in her for the last two years—or more
if she was honest—rose up like a river after a rainstorm.

She tugged her hand back and stepped away. "Let me
show you another book I plan to work on." She reached
for a black leather volume, its pages coming loose from
the worn binding. Her hands trembled as she heaved its
weight toward Vasco, anxious to break the seductive
spell he seemed to have cast over her.

She didn't dare look at him but she imagined his
eyes laughing. He knew how much power he had over
her and he found it amusing. Flirtation came naturally
to him and he used it like a weapon. She'd better find

some good armor, possibly the polished set of inlaid sixteenth century armor in the great hall. That looked about her size.

"What's so funny?" His voice tickled her ears.

"Just wondering how I'd look in a suit of armor."

"It's easy to find out. I used to try them on myself when I was a kid—even rode my horse in one, which wasn't too comfortable." He laughed. "But none of them fit me now. Our ancestors were smaller than we are." His daring eyes swept over her again. "Though you're about the right size for Francesca's. Come on."

He'd been leaning on the table with one hip, but he rose and headed for the door, beckoning her.

Stella swallowed. Did he really intend for her to try on some armor? She had to admit the idea had some appeal. How often did you have an opportunity to peek into the experiences of people in another era? Now she'd know how a nervous eighteen-year-old count might feel as he dressed for battle with a neighboring fiefdom.

Her pace quickened as she followed him. She wasn't exactly dressed for battle, medieval or otherwise. Her long dress swept around her legs as she hurried down the hallway. Would he expect her to take it off? Karen had convinced her to buy new lingerie for her trip on the pretext that if servants would be arranging her belongings, they should fit in with a royal household, not scream "bargain bin."

She wasn't sure how many royal guests wore skimpy pale silver satin and lace, but at least her underwear drawer did look smart and she felt glamorous when she put them on.

Vasco led her along a gloomy passageway, il-luminated by a single lamp, and into a vast chamber with no lighting of any kind. He flicked a switch and spotlights in the ceiling splashed over a startling display of weaponry arranged on the walls in intricate patterns. Swords crisscrossed each other and muskets fanned out like lace petticoats. Armaments covered most of three walls, shining and polished as if ready for immediate use.

"My ancestors liked to keep their defenses at hand." Vasco grinned. "But they also liked things to be pretty."

"Does someone take these down to polish them?"

"Only once a year. They haven't been pressed into service for quite some time."

"That's a relief. Besides, it can't be easy to buy ammunition for a seventeenth century musket these days."

"You'd be surprised…" he winked "…at what you can find on eBay."

Spotlights also illuminated three suits of armor, each standing in a corner. Two were silver metal with tooled decoration, the other was black and bronze, very elaborate and slightly smaller than the others.

"It's so pretty." She walked toward the unusual one. "Is it Italian?"

"It is." He sounded surprised that she knew. "My ancestor Francesc Turmeda Montoya had it made in Genoa and brought here over the mountains. By the time it arrived he'd grown and it didn't fit."

"What a waste. So it was never worn?"

"Not by him. I'd imagine it was pressed into service over the years from time to time." His long, strong fingers caressed the tooled metal. "But it's possible that it's never experienced the pleasure of encasing a woman's body."

Stella felt every inch a woman as Vasco's gaze met hers. "It does look like it might fit."

He reached behind the torso and unbuckled something. The breastplate, arms still attached, loosened from the stand. "I think you'd better slip out of your dress."

Stella fought the urge to laugh. "What if someone comes?"

"They won't."

"What if war breaks out and all the staff comes running to find the weapons?"

"Then you'll be dressed for battle." His dimples deepened. "Let me help you." He pulled his hands away from the armor and stepped behind her. The sound of her zipper sliding down her back made tiny hairs stand on end all over her body. She shrugged out of the arms and let the dress slide to the floor.

"Lucky thing I'm not self-conscious," she said, wishing she really wasn't. At least the spotlights focused on the armaments, so she stood in relative shadow outside the pool of light on the armor.

She glanced at Vasco to find his eyes feasting unashamedly on her bare skin. Her nipples thickened inside her elegant bra and she felt an urgent need to hide behind the black and gold metal. "Hold it out for me."

He lifted the breastplate off the stand. The arms clanked against the torso with a sound that could wake the dead, and she glanced behind her before sliding her arms into the dark holes and letting Vasco step behind her to fasten the straps. His fingers brushed her back as he closed the armor and she tried not to shiver.

The legs fastened individually, strapping over her thighs and attaching to the main body, so Vasco's fingers had a lot of intimate contact with her skin. The mere touch of his hands made her breath catch at the bottom of her lungs. At last she was entirely encased in metal except her head. "Let's see if I can walk." She felt precarious. The armor was heavy and with her hands in metal gauntlets she wasn't sure she could catch herself if she fell.

"You look like a very elegant Joan of Arc."

She took a tentative step forward. Surprisingly, the armor moved with her like a second, if heavyweight, skin, though the shoe part was too large and clanked on the stone floor. "It's not easy to walk in these things."

"That's why you need a horse." Vasco smiled. "No one marched into battle in that getup. Want to try the helmet?" He lifted the tooled headpiece.

Stella nodded, and let Vasco lower it over her head. She'd worn her hair loose tonight, curling around her neck, and she tucked in the bottom ends so they wouldn't stick out. It was dark inside the helmet, and had an interesting smell, more like wood than metal. She wondered about the people who'd stood in here before. Were they preparing for battle and fighting their fears, or were they like her, just trying it on for fun?

She couldn't see Vasco at all. The eye slits weren't quite in the right place so she could only see the floor and up to his knees. They must work better up on a horse.

She pulled off the helmet, and even the spare illumination in the armaments chamber seemed blinding after the darkness inside. "Phew. It's nice to be able to breathe again. I can picture you riding around the countryside carrying a lance. Rescuing a fair maiden or two."

One dark brow lifted. "What makes you think I would be rescuing them?"

"Okay, endangering their virtue."

"Probably closer to the truth." Even the way the skin around his eyes crinkled only made him more handsome. "But I would mean well." His seductive smile and tilted head seemed to gently ask forgiveness.

"I'll bet." Even in the armor she didn't feel at all safe around Vasco. And it was getting uncomfortably hot in here. "I'd better get this off."

Vasco's slow smile crept across his mouth again. "Let me help you with that."

Six

Vasco had noticed that Stella's hair changed color depending on the light. Right now the spotlight that usually shone on the armor picked out bright gold and red strands from the silky bob.

Sweet and excited but slightly hesitant, her smile tormented him. Her pink lips were mobile, soft and tempting. He could almost imagine how it would feel to kiss her.

But not quite. There was only one way to find out what her mouth would feel like pressed against his.

His knuckles caressed her back as he unbuckled the armor. Soft and warm, her skin begged to be touched. The clasp on her bra beckoned him like the key to a hidden chamber, and with difficulty he managed to prevent himself from unlocking it.

Stella slid out of the armor and he lifted it back onto its armature, irked that he had to drag his eyes from the inviting vision of her body. Luckily the legs required some assistance to remove. The darkness hid his appreciative gaze as he released her deliciously athletic thighs from their metal casing, and pulled the heavy shoes from her delicate feet with their coral-tipped toes.

Her silky underwear didn't help matters. It took all his self-control not to cup the sweet roundness of her backside. Instead he held up her dress and helped her back into it. Her cheeks were pink, even in the dim light. He'd like to see them flushed deeper, with exertion and desire.

Good things come to those who wait.

"I enjoyed that." She fastened the matching belt back around her waist. "Although it's heavy, it's also surprisingly flexible. I'd never have imagined that."

"This armor was cutting-edge technology in its time. No expense would have been spared in kitting out the son and heir to defend the family lands and honor and live to tell the tale."

Stella's eyes looked golden in the half-light of the chamber. "Do you wish you'd lived back then?"

"What man wouldn't?"

"The ones who'd rather play battle games on a computer, I suppose."

"I don't have the patience for those. I'd rather feel the blood pulsing in my veins."

"Or pulsing right out of them if it was a real battle. I'm glad Nicky won't be expected to ride into battle on a galloping horse. That would scare the life out of me."

"I'd imagine mothers have felt the same throughout history." He picked up her hand, an instinctive gesture.

"However, they haven't often had the final say in such matters."

She raised a brow. "Luckily women do have an equal say now. At least in civilized countries." He saw the glint of a challenge in her eyes.

"I suppose it remains to be seen whether Montmajor is civilized in your eyes." He couldn't keep a smile from his lips. "Though it's a hard thing to quantify. We do bathe somewhat regularly and use utensils at the table."

"I'll make up my own mind." A smile tugged at her soft, pink mouth. "I certainly have my doubts about their king."

"I imagine a lot of people do." He loved that she wasn't intimidated by his titles and all the pomp and circumstance that came with them. "I do my best to convince them that under this rough exterior beats a heart of gold."

Her laugh bounced off the weapon-laden walls and filled the air with its soft music. "No one could accuse you of being modest."

"Modesty is not a quality people seek in their king." He let his hungry eyes feast for a moment on Stella's delicious body. Her dress wrapped snugly around her waist, then flared out, concealing the curve of her hips and those silky thighs. Lucky thing the memory of them—and her seductively elegant underwear—was imprinted on his brain like a freshly switched-off lightbulb.

"I suppose arrogance and a sense of entitlement are more appropriate to a monarch." She lifted her neat chin.

"But only in measured doses, otherwise people might

want to rise up and overthrow me." He grinned. "We don't want them storming the castle."

"No, it would take too long to get all these weapons down off the wall."

"Don't worry. The palace staff is trained in kung fu."

"Really?"

"No." He took her hand and kissed it. Couldn't help himself. He knew it would be soft and warm and feel sensational against his lips.

The color in her cheeks deepened. She was ready. He could tell she was interested. Hell, he'd seen the first sparks of it in her eyes during his first surprise visit, somewhere behind the alarm and fear. Now she'd had time to get to know him and his world a little, to relax and realize that he wanted the best for her and Nicky. Even if she was still wary, she was open-minded and prepared to like both him and his country.

Now he needed to apply a little glue.

He stepped toward her and her eyes widened. Before she had a chance to move, he cupped her head with his free hand and kissed her gently but firmly on the lips.

She tasted fresh, like summer wine. A jolt of arousal crashed through him, and his fingers sank into the softness of her hair. His tongue slid between her lips, prying them open, and he longed to press his body against hers.

But two small hands on his chest pushed him back.

He blinked, aching as the intoxicating kiss came to an abrupt end.

"I don't think we should do this." Stella sounded breathless. Her eyes sparkled with a mix of shock and arousal. "Things are so complicated already."

"Then let's make them simple." He stroked her cheek. The hot, flushed skin begged to be cooled by kisses.

"This doesn't make anything simple. We barely know each other."

"We share the strongest bond any man and woman can enjoy—a child."

"That's what worries me. We owe it to Nicky to keep things harmonious between us. Once…romance comes into the picture, that's when problems start."

"Has that been your experience?" He raised a brow. Maybe she was single with good reason.

"I was in a long relationship that I ultimately decided wasn't what I wanted."

"What made you decide that?"

She hesitated, blinked. "Partly, at least, because he didn't want children."

He smiled. "So, problem solved in this case." Her mouth looked so lush, and now that he'd tasted it he couldn't bear to simply look at it.

"But what if we decide we hate each other?"

"Impossible."

"So you think we'll just kiss and live happily ever after?"

"Why not?" Happily ever after was an awfully long time, but the sight of her tempting body a few hot inches away made him ready to promise almost anything. He liked Stella immensely. She'd gone to a lot of trouble to come here and adjust herself to Montmajor for Nicky's sake and his sake, and he could tell she was a woman with a big heart as well as a lovely face.

"Why not?" She blew out a sharp breath. "I'd love to live in a world of fairy tales but reality does keep poking its ugly head back up. What will the other people at the palace say?"

"Who cares? I'm the king. I don't trouble myself with the thoughts of other people." He grinned. He hadn't troubled himself all that much with them when he wasn't king, either, but no need to mention that.

He trailed his fingers down her neck and to her shoulder. Her collarbone disappeared into the pretty aqua dress and he followed it with his fingertips. Stella shivered slightly, and he watched her chest rise and fall.

She wanted him.

His own arousal strained uncomfortably against his pants. His need to seduce her into bed tonight was becoming urgent. He slid his arms around her waist. "Trust your instincts."

"My instincts are telling me to run a mile." The smile dancing around the corners of her mouth made him doubt her statement.

"No, that's some silly part of your brain that wants to prevent you from enjoying too much pleasure."

"Is it really?" Her eyes twinkled.

Almost there.

"Absolutely. You need to switch it off."

"How do I do that?" She raised a brow.

"Like this." He pulled her close and pressed his lips to hers again, this time deepening the kiss right away, enjoying the hot softness of her mouth with his tongue.

Her arms rose around his neck and he felt her sink into his embrace. A tiny sigh rose in her throat as their bodies bumped together, her nipples brushed against his chest through the fabric of their clothes. He let his hands roam lower, to enjoy the curve of her backside and thigh.

Stella writhed against him, pulling him closer, her hot cheek against his and her eyes closed tight. Desire built inside him almost to the boiling point as her lush body tempted him into a state of rock-hard arousal.

With great difficulty he pulled back an inch or two. It was time to transfer this scene to a room with a comfortable surface of some kind. Like a bed.

"Come with me." He was half-tempted to pick her up and carry her, to reduce the chance of her changing her mind, but he managed to resist. Holding her hand tightly, he led her out of the armaments chamber and up the flight of stairs into the east tower.

He'd ordered fresh sheets for the round bedroom in happy anticipation of this moment. With windows on all sides, but no one outside to see in, this room was the most private in the whole palace and had no doubt been used for royal trysts for hundreds of years.

He pushed open the door and was pleased to see a vase filled with fresh flowers glowing under an already lit lamp. The grand hangings on the bed shone, the embroidery shimmering with gold thread, and the covers were turned back to reveal soft, freshly laundered linen.

"What a lovely room." Stella hesitated in the doorway. "It's not your bedroom, is it?" She'd seen him change clothes in his own bedroom.

"It's *our* bedroom." He pulled her into his arms and shoved the door closed behind them with his foot, then drew her into a kiss that silenced all thought, let alone conversation.

Stella couldn't believe she was able to kiss Vasco and breathe at the same time, but it must be happening because the kiss went on and on, drawing her deeper into a sensual trance.

She'd never experienced anything like this kiss. Sensation cascaded through her, bringing every inch of her alive and making her aware of her body in an entirely new way. Colors danced behind her eyelids and her fingers and toes tingled with awareness as Vasco's tongue jousted with hers.

When he finally pulled back—she would have been totally unable to—she emerged blinking and breathless back into reality like a creature startled out of hibernation.

So *this* is what people made such a fuss about. She'd always wondered about the poems and songs and all the drama surrounding romance and sex. Her own love life had been prosaic enough that she thought they were all exaggerating for effect. Now she could see she'd been missing out on the more exciting aspects of the experience.

And they hadn't even had sex yet...

Vasco's eyes shone with passion that mirrored her own and electricity crackled in the air around them. This was the chemistry people talked about, she could feel it like an explosive reaction about to happen, heating her blood and stirring her senses into a witches' brew of excitement.

Vasco reached behind him and switched off the light. A fat pale-gold moon hung outside the windows, bathing them both in its soft glow, turning the dramatic round room into a magical space.

Her hands were buried in the soft cotton of Vasco's shirt, clutching at the muscle beneath. She longed to pull the fabric from his body, but some vestige of modesty prevented her. Vasco had no such scruples. He undid the tie that held the waist of her dress together and unwrapped her like a gift. For the second time that night her dress descended to the floor and she stood before him in her underwear. This time, however, she had no armor to hide in.

His eyes roamed over her body, heating her skin with their warm admiration. His fingers followed, stirring currents of sensation wherever they touched. She let herself move under his hands, enjoying their sensual touch as she ran her fingers over his shirt, feeling the muscle beneath.

Soon enough her fingers found themselves plucking the buttons from their holes and pushing the fabric back over his shoulders. She'd had a glimpse of Vasco's chest earlier—surely that was his real bedroom?—and it was even firmer and more enticing at close range. A shadow of dark hair disappeared into his belt buckle, and soon she found herself sliding the leather out of it and unzipping his black pants.

It was glaringly obvious that he was every bit as aroused as her. His erection jutted against his briefs. She let her knuckles graze against it as she pushed his pants down past his thighs, and the hardness of it made her shiver. Trevor had always needed a good deal of coaxing to get ready, by which point her interest had sometimes waned. Clearly Vasco did not need any encouragement.

She glanced up at his face, and his predatory gaze only deepened the intensity of her desire. His lips were parted and she could feel his breathing, watch his chest rise and fall as anticipation jumped between them like a spark. Her own heart thumped so loud she could almost hear it in the still nighttime silence. It grew louder and faster as Vasco reached around her back and unhooked her bra.

She could pretend it was the cool night air that tightened her nipples, but they both knew better. Vasco lowered his head and licked one, then looked up at her, eyes shining with desire. She pushed his underwear down and he kicked it away. Glazed with moonlight, his hard body looked like an ancient statue. She could hardly believe such a gorgeous vision was interested in her.

Vasco plucked at her scanty lace briefs, then slid them down her thighs, leaving them both naked. The moonlight felt like a warm robe around her, making her unselfconscious and hungry for the feel of his body against hers. She stepped forward, until the tips of her breasts brushed his chest. The tickling sensation almost made her laugh and step back, but Vasco's big hands caught her around the waist and pulled her closer.

Their bellies met, Vasco's fierce arousal trapped between them. He captured her mouth in a kiss that made her head spin and ran his fingers through her hair. Stella's hands wandered over his muscled back, enjoying the athletic perfection of his body as the pressure of their desire built between them like water held behind a dam.

Stella felt the soft edge of the mattress behind her thighs, and realized they'd been moving backward to the bed. Vasco's hands cupped her buttocks and lifted her onto the high surface, without breaking their kiss. The soft fabric felt cool beneath her hot skin, and she wriggled a little, enjoying the sensation. Vasco laid her backward, easing himself over her. He pulled back enough to look into her eyes. "You're a very sensual woman."

"Who knew?" She sounded as surprised as she felt. Her senses were alight with wonder and excitement she'd never imagined. She'd not given sex more than a passing thought in so long she almost wondered if she'd ever have it again. Or if she even cared.

Now she craved it like her next breath.

Vasco slid into her slowly and she arched her back to take him deep. A groan of sheer pleasure slid from her lips and flew into his mouth as it covered hers again. He moved with creativity and elegance, shifting his body over hers and drawing her closer into a tangle of delight.

As they writhed together on the bed, she felt like the partner of an expert dancer who knew how to bring out her own innate talent. She found herself guiding them, too, climbing on top to deepen the dramatic sensations coursing through her, then letting him tilt her body to daring angles and roll with her in perfectly executed moments that made her gasp for breath as passion crashed through her.

Vasco's warm skin against hers felt so right. His arms around her waist or her shoulders, his fingers in her hair or caressing the skin of her face, every touch was gloriously perfect. When her climax reached the point of no return she let herself disappear into the ecstatic madness of the moment, clinging to him while the real world fell away.

In his arms afterward, wrung out by the intensity of the experience, she could barely remember her name or even breathe. His mouth and hands and tongue had explored every inch of her, making her whole body quiver with desire and anticipation, then giving her satisfaction she'd never known before. Now she felt soft and pliable, relaxed and content. Happy.

Vasco whispered to her, sometimes in English, sometimes in Catalan, telling her how beautiful she was, what a sensual lover, what a fantastic mother and how pleased he was to have her here in Montmajor. And in his bed.

Everything he said seemed normal and natural and made her smile though she could rarely summon the energy to reply. That didn't seem to matter. She rested her head on the firm pillow of his chest and drifted off to sleep, lulled by the rhythm of his big heart.

Her dreams were surreal visions of their imagined life in the palace. Walking, laughing and talking together. The perfect happy family living a comfortable and enjoyable life amidst the sandstone walls of a thousand-year-old castle. Normal and natural and predictable as the sunrise—which poked its bright harsh fingers through all those windows around the room and jolted her from sleep with alarming suddenness.

Only then did she realize what she'd done.

Seven

Stella sat up in bed and raised a hand to keep the bright sun out of her eyes. A quick glance at the pillow next to hers confirmed that Vasco was gone. When had he left? Did he sleep with her all night or disappear the moment she fell asleep?

Had he used a condom? She hadn't spared a thought for contraception. Trevor had always been the one to worry about that, since he was so terrified of having children and the responsibility and expense it would entail. He'd always come armed with condoms despite the fact he'd convinced her to have an IUD fitted. She'd had the IUD removed to conceive Nicky, and hadn't bothered with birth control since because she hadn't been on a single date.

She swallowed. Her insides still pulsed with traces of the fierce contractions she'd enjoyed at the peak of their lovemaking. Vasco had turned her inside and out, guiding her to feats of sexual acrobatics that made her blink as she remembered them. Wow. Who knew there was a whole new world of sexual pleasure out there that she'd barely even dipped her toes in?

Now she'd dived in headfirst, with a man she barely knew, who just happened to be the father of her son.

She climbed out of bed, scanning the room for her clothes. Light blazed in through the windows, leaving her naked and exposed. She found her dress in a crumpled heap on the floor, and her skimpy lingerie under the bed, where it must have been kicked by eager feet. She fished them out and tugged them back on with shaky hands.

How easy it had been for Vasco to seduce her. Her face heated. She hadn't even been here a week. Or all of three days. She'd leaped into bed with him the first time he even kissed her.

Her dress was crumpled, but she pulled it on and fastened the tie at the waist. She'd wanted him to see her as attractive, desirable. She didn't want him to think that the woman who'd bought his sperm was someone who couldn't find a man the old-fashioned way. Had she bent over backwards to convince herself she could tempt Vasco?

She certainly had put effort into looking nice and attempting to be a charming guest. He must know she wanted him to like her, and now he'd obliged by taking her to bed.

The large four-poster bed with its long curtains loomed over her. Whose bed was this? Not Vasco's, for sure. Was this room reserved for sexual escapades with visiting women? There were no signs of habitation, no pictures or bits of clothing or toiletries. It looked like a museum recreation of an ancient castle bedroom. Except that it was the real thing.

The sun had just lifted over the horizon, so hopefully Nicky was still asleep, but what if he'd woken up in the night, wanting her? He could have been calling for her for hours and no one knew where she was.

Heartbeat quickening, she picked up her shoes from under a chair and hurried to the door. Hopefully most of the staff was still asleep and she could sneak back to her room without being seen.

She pulled open the tall, heavy wood door and peered outside. The lightless hallway looked like a black hole after the blinding light of dawn illuminating the bedroom. She hadn't paid close attention on the way here, so she wasn't even sure which part of the palace she was in.

The cold stone stung her feet as she tiptoed into a narrow corridor which led to a flight of spiral stone stairs heading up and down. She went down, and out through the next arched doorway into a small courtyard where dew clung to ornate iron railings. Had she come this way last night? She'd been so wrapped up in Vasco she hadn't noticed. No doubt she'd assumed he'd be escorting her back, as well.

She should have known better than to think Vasco so predictable.

The courtyard had two doors leading out the other side, and she picked the one on the right, only to find it locked. The door on the left was open, and she crept through it with relief, but didn't recognize the wide hall she found herself in. A large, rather faded tapestry covered one wall, and an ancient wooden chair stood in one corner. There were doors at both ends, but no clue which one led to the busier part of the castle.

Stella hurried to the nearest door and peeped through it. It scraped on the floor as she pushed it open a crack and her heart almost stopped when she found herself peering into what was obviously a chapel. Tall candles burned on a small altar and the smell of incense wafted from a censer above it. The morning sun lit up a series of jewellike stained-glass windows, strung amid carved columns like stones in a necklace.

Worse yet, three black-clothed bodies knelt at the altar—the "aunts"—deep in morning prayer. She shrank back from the door, but it was too late. One of them—Lilli—had already turned.

"Stella." Her voice rang through the sacred space, rooting Stella to the spot like one of the carved statues above the altar.

Shoes in hand, she felt her face flush purple as all three heads turned to stare at her.

"Come join us for Matins." For the first time she noticed the priest, a shadowy figure near the altar. Was this the right time to explain that she'd been raised Lutheran? She gulped and smiled. She was probably supposed to cross herself or curtsy or some of the things she'd seen in films, but right now she just wanted to die.

"Sorry, wrong room." She backed away, shame pulsing through her veins, hoping they hadn't seen too much of her crumpled dress. Maybe they wouldn't put two and two together. What kind of woman would they think her if they knew she'd slept with Vasco on her second night at the palace?

She ran a hand through her tangled hair and scurried in the opposite direction, where she found herself in the great armaments chamber, facing the suit of armor she'd so readily stripped to don last night. What happened to her when Vasco was around? Normally she was a modest and reasonably sensible person.

Footsteps on the stone outside the room made her sink into a corner. Luckily the spotlights were turned off and she pressed herself against the wall beside a polished silver suit of armor until the sound disappeared into the distance.

This time she put her shoes on before venturing out again. At least then she could pretend she was up and dressed—if inappropriately—for the day, rather than creeping about in last night's rumpled finery. She found her way back to the suite she shared with Nicky without too much trouble. The door to Nicky's adjoining room was open and the sitter—a girl who worked in events planning—was asleep in an armchair next to the bed. Stella cringed at the realization that at least this one person would know exactly what she'd been up to last night.

Nicky was still sweetly asleep in the bed they'd made up for him, clutching the dinosaur Vasco gave him.

I'm so sorry, Nicky. I don't know what I was thinking. What happened last night would certainly complicate things. Would it develop into some kind of romantic relationship? Or was it just a one night fling?

The latter would be awful. She'd rather not have known how astonishing and enjoyable good sex could be. And the thought of not being able to kiss Vasco again…

She shook her head, trying to clear it, as she walked back into her room. For now she had to keep going. She ruffled the bed, as if she'd just climbed out of it, then went into the adjoining bathroom for a shower. She almost laughed but the sight of her flushed face and wild hair in the mirror made it shrivel in her throat.

Everyone would know. And she couldn't help thinking that's exactly what Vasco intended. He'd been hugging her and fondling her and flirting with her since they got here, apparently keen for people to think they were an item. Maybe he didn't want anyone to find out that he donated the royal seed to a sperm bank. That wouldn't go over too well with his devout Catholic "aunties."

Stella climbed into the stream of steamy water and wished she could scrub away her guilt and embarrassment at being so quick to jump into bed with him. He started it!

This time she did laugh, and when she emerged from the shower, she felt much better. She was also relieved to see that the sitter had left, so who knew, maybe her rumpled sheet ruse could have worked, too?

She took Nicky down for breakfast, hoping to finish quickly and go hide among the books—even though that would mean facing the "aunts" again so she could place Nicky in their care—before Vasco came down. She gulped hard when she saw him sitting at the table, biting into a slice of melon.

He rose to his feet with a mischievous smile when she entered. He held her gaze just a little longer than appropriate, then glanced down at Nicky and said something in Catalan.

Nicky smiled. "*Hola,* Papa."

Stella stared at him. Now he was saying complete sentences in a foreign language? Not to mention calling this virtual stranger Dad. Vasco grinned, those inviting dimples puckering his tanned skin.

"Come join me." He gestured at the chair beside his for Stella. "I bet you're hungry." His eyes flashed in a way that made her belly quiver and her face heat. Was he trying to embarrass her? Probably not. He was just being Vasco.

She rounded the table, still holding Nicky's hand, and settled him into the chair next to Vasco. Better to have some distance between them. As soon as the child was seated, however, Vasco moved up to her and pressed his lips to hers. Too startled to protest, she found herself kissing him right over Nicky's head. Desire roared to life inside her, and she was blinking and breathless when she finally managed to pull back.

She couldn't help glancing nervously about to see if any of the staff were there.

"You look radiant."

Hopefully that's not because I'm pregnant. Now was not the time to ask if he'd used anything, though. She was furious with him for kissing her in front of Nicky— not that he'd noticed—and anyone else who might walk in.

"I'm not sure what got into me," she murmured, avoiding his gaze.

"I am." His secretive smile only stoked the infuriating fires burning inside her. He handed her a plate of fruit. "You need to rebuild your strength."

"My stamina is just fine, thank you." She took a seat on the far side of Nicky and primly spread her napkin on her lap.

"I'm tempted to make you prove it." He took another

bite of melon, sinking his teeth in with obvious gusto. The gesture made her hips wriggle.

How could he carry on like this in front of his own innocent son? Obviously the man had no scruples. She reached for a piece of toasted muffin from a plate in the center of the table and spread it with butter. Vasco chattered away to Nicky in Catalan as if they were having a conversation. Stella almost dropped her knife when Nicky replied, "*Sì*, Papa."

"Nicky, that's fantastic. You're learning to speak a new language."

"Of course he is." Vasco rubbed Nicky's blond hair, messing it up. "It's his native tongue."

"He does seem to be picking it up surprisingly fast. He barely said a word until this month."

"Because he was speaking the wrong language." He spoke to Nicky again in Catalan. Stella couldn't make out what he said, but Nicky laughed.

A knot formed in her stomach and she realized she felt left out. Which was ridiculous. She could learn Catalan, too, even if it wasn't intricately woven into her DNA.

"Today I'll take Nicky for a tour of the town while you work on your books." Vasco took another bite of melon. It was a declaration rather than a suggestion.

She tensed. "He might get anxious being away from me."

"Don't worry. If he fusses I'll bring him right back." He stroked Nicky's tiny chin with his thumb and spooned in a mouthful of Nicky's favorite oatmeal that one of the staff had magically appeared with. "And we'll come play with your books."

"Great. Bring some crayons. Nicky can decorate you with gold leaf."

"I like that idea. This shirt is a bit dull." He glanced down at his well-cut black shirt. "But we'll let you get some work done first."

Why did she trust him completely with Nicky? She wanted to be nervous, or suspicious, but it was hard. She knew that most of the reservations she had concerned herself, not Nicky.

And if this morning's kiss was anything to go by, last night was not a one-night stand.

A week later, little had changed. Nicky was now babbling complete nursery rhymes in Catalan. Stella had plenty of time to lose herself in the demanding but exhilarating world of the ancient library. And she'd slept with Vasco every night.

They always slept in the same room. She'd asked again whose room it was, and he always replied that it was "theirs." Vasco was never there when she awoke. Her feelings on this had developed from surprise into disappointment, but she didn't like to whine about it. They'd only been involved for one week, so she was hardly in a position to ask him to adjust his lifestyle to her needs. Or maybe she didn't want to make waves when she enjoyed their time together so much. Now at least she knew the way back to her room.

During the day Vasco was flirtatious and affectionate, treating her like his lover, regardless of who was around. They'd even strolled through the town with Nicky twice, as if they were a real family.

Stella's ears burned all the time. She could imagine the gossip that must result when the nation's dashing young king showed up with a woman and child and no wedding ring in sight. The "aunts" said nothing, just smiled sweetly and doted over Nicky. The staff members were polite and somewhat deferent, treating her as a guest rather than one of themselves, though theoretically at least she was there to do a job.

And there was no discussion about the future. Vasco seemed to operate under the assumption that she and Nicky were there for good, and since it was too early to decide whether they were or not, she didn't ask any pointed questions. Most of the time they were together they were either within earshot of the staff, at dinner for example, or in bed. Neither was the ideal place for a "state of the state" conversation.

The moment Vasco kissed her, all practical concerns melted away and she floated on a cloud of bliss that could be temporary or eternal, her mind and body didn't seem to care. The palace was like a little country in its own right and—busy with Nicky and Vasco and the library—she almost forgot about the rest of the world chugging along all around them.

So it was a rude awakening when a former work colleague in L.A. sent her an abrupt email with the heading "OMG Stella—this you?" and a link to *CelebCrush* magazine's website. Stella clicked the link wondering if she had a job lead. She and the sender had been out for lunch a few times and she knew Elaine, an archivist, had found a new position at the Getty Museum.

The link took her to a headline blaring "Royal Romance?" The tone of the article was breathless. "Dashing King of Montmajor Vasco Montoya has been spotted out on the town with a mysterious

American—and her young child. Rumors are buzzing that he's the dad. Royal mistress, or future wife?" Stella blinked. There was a large picture of her and Vasco, each of them holding one of Nicky's hands, as they walked past a fruit stall in the main square of the town. She was staring at Vasco with a goofy grin on her face, while he looked boldly ahead, all windswept good looks and photogenic charm.

There wasn't any more to the story. Apparently that's what passed for journalism at *CelebCrush* magazine. Not that there was much more to the story in real life.

Her heart pounded beneath her neat yellow blouse as she sat in the library in full view of the elderly caretaker who dusted the volumes daily. Who else might see this? She was tempted to email back, "Nope, not me!" but she couldn't.

Royal mistress or future wife? Cringeworthy. What if Vasco saw this? She clicked away from the page and back to her Yahoo! homepage. At least she'd never heard of this magazine. A little research told her it was based out of Luxembourg, and for all she knew had a circulation of about twenty-five. Still, the fact that Elaine had stumbled across the website out in California was a bit alarming, since she hadn't mentioned Vasco to anyone except her best friend, Karen. She'd told other friends and neighbors she was taking Nicky to Europe for a vacation.

She typed back the words "Out of office autoreply— Stella is busy sleeping with a European monarch, and will attend to your email as soon as possible. Until then, please mind your own business." She wanted to laugh hysterically. Or cry. Then she deleted it all except the first phrase, wrote a more prosaic version and sent it out right away. That at least would keep Elaine from asking for more details.

She slammed the laptop and hurried from the library, unable to sit still, let alone do delicate restoration work. Maybe it was time to ask Vasco where this whole thing was going. It might be nice to know the answer for when a reporter thrust a microphone in her face.

At least she wasn't likely to be pregnant. He'd used condoms on all the subsequent trysts so she probably just hadn't noticed him rolling it deftly on in the excitement of their first encounter.

"Stella." Vasco's voice behind her stopped her in her tracks. "Where are you rushing?" He walked up behind her and slid his arms around her waist. Her belly shuddered with awareness. "To find me, I hope." His deep voice curled into her ear. It was hard to think straight and be practical around Vasco.

"Can we talk about something?" She drew in a breath, trying to steady her nerves.

"We can talk about anything. Astrophysics, the Holy Grail, the works of J.D. Salinger, what to eat for lunch…" He pressed a kiss to the back of her neck and she felt her knees turn to jelly.

"Let's go somewhere private."

"An excellent idea. Let's go to our room."

"No, somewhere without a bed." She couldn't stop the smile that tugged at her mouth even as she spun around to extricate herself from his embrace.

"Tired of beds?" A piratical grin lit his features. "Then we'll head outside. Follow me." He hooked his arm through hers and marched her along the corridor. They exited the palace through a side door and headed down a long, curving flight of stairs onto the hillside below the castle walls.

Grassy hills dotted with sheep and cattle unfurled around them like a rumpled blanket. "Where are we going?" She was glad she wore ballet flats, not heels, as they set out on a narrow track.

"Nowhere." Vasco marched ahead, holding her hand. "Which is one of my favorite places."

"Oh." Now would be a good time for discussion. Nicky was with two of the "aunts" and almost due for his nap, so he wouldn't miss her if she was gone for a while. She cleared her throat. "I'm a little confused about my status here."

"Really? Right now I'd say you're walking." He flashed that pearly grin before turning around to stride ahead again.

"Very funny. I mean the status of me and you."

"Intimate, definitely." He squeezed her hand.

"I know that, but am I..." How did you put this stuff without sounding like a middle schooler? "...your girlfriend?"

"Most definitely."

"Oh." Relief filled her chest. So they were dating. That was something she could understand.

"And much more than that. You're the mother of my child. We're a family." His dark gaze was meaningful, serious.

The complicated part again. Vasco seemed to assume that Nicky tied them together permanently, no matter what else happened. Which he did, of course, but did that mean they were going to get married?

On less than a month's acquaintance she wasn't brave

enough to ask that. Did she even want to marry him and abandon her freewheeling single life?

Yes, of course she did. Her heart sank as she realized how much she'd fallen in love with him in such a short time. He'd swept her right off her sensible shoes and deposited her here in his fairy kingdom, where he spent hours seducing her to shocking new heights and depths of sensual pleasure. Montmajor was a peaceful and lovely place, with seemingly no poverty or social unrest, and was less than two hours by plane to nearly every capital in Europe. And then there was a lifetime of satisfying work—probably several lifetimes, in fact—restoring all those magnificent books.

But did Vasco intend to make her his queen, or was the "royal mistress" scenario more realistic?

In her heart, she knew the answer. "Why don't we sleep in my room or your room? Why the round chamber?"

"That's a special place just for us."

"But my bedroom is lovely, and I wouldn't need anyone to listen for Nicky overnight if we were right next door."

"You might get tired of finding me in your bed."

Or you might get tired of me. "Why do you always leave in the night?" She'd never dared to ask before.

Vasco squeezed her hand again, still walking. "I do business in Asia, and that's the best time to make phone calls. I wouldn't want to disturb you."

She frowned. It was a good reason, but not entirely convincing. "I can sleep through anything, you really don't need to leave."

"It's easier if I'm in my office." He picked up the

pace a bit as they climbed a small hill, and she had to struggle to keep up. "It's all quite tiresome."

"If it was tiresome, you wouldn't do it. I know you too well already."

He laughed. "Okay, I enjoy my businesses. I can't just sit around on the throne all day gassing with the citizens. I need new challenges."

That's what worries me.

The round room with all its windows was their room—which he could leave at any time to take up in a different room with someone else.

"Is the palace always this quiet? I mean, do you not have to entertain foreign dignitaries and that kind of thing?"

Vasco slowed. "I didn't want to scare you off by thrusting you into the middle of a social whirl, so I told my events planner to keep things light while you settled in. Are you ready for some more excitement?"

"Um, I don't know." She wasn't wild about the prospect of being surrounded by medal-laden dignitaries or glossy-haired princesses. What would they think of a simple girl from suburban L.A.?

She straightened her back. She didn't have anything to be embarrassed about. She was educated and intelligent and could hold a conversation. As an American, she wasn't intimidated by blue blood or piles of wealth. It would be interesting to meet different people. "Sure, why not?"

At a social event he'd have to introduce her as something. Then maybe she'd know where she stood. *My fiancée,* perhaps?

"Then we'll send out some invitations." Vasco

raised a brow. "Though I admit I'd rather keep you all to myself."

He pulled her gently along with him as they climbed another small slope, then they paused at the top. The view was incredible. Hills and mountains all around, including the castle-topped one behind them. There was no sign of civilization.

Stella stared around them. Not even a distant plane in the sky. "I feel like we're all alone in the world." The sun glazed peaks and valleys with pale gold light.

"We are, for now." Vasco's strong features glowed in the warm light.

For now. Those words rang a little ominous in her ears. She'd asked her question about her status and received an answer. She was his girlfriend as well as the mother of his child.

That would just have to do. For now.

She'd been here barely a week, so who was she to start making demands and asking pointed questions when she didn't even know what she wanted. She might tire of Vasco and Montmajor and decide to head home, so it didn't make sense to demand a commitment from him when she wasn't ready to offer one herself.

Why was it so hard to be patient and let events evolve naturally? They'd just started dating. Okay, so it was a little more intense than usual since they lived under the same roof—and had a son—but any relationship was a delicate thing that could suffocate and die under too much pressure. She needed to relax and go with the flow a bit, enjoy the moment, live in the present and let their relationship grow in its own way.

Eight

Nicky was safely tucked up in bed when the first guests arrived. Stella had spent hours getting ready, or at least it seemed like hours. She'd bought a new dress and shoes in the town, with a credit card Vasco gave her and told her to "enjoy." She felt appallingly self-conscious flicking through racks of dresses at the local boutique under the watchful eye of the proprietor, who must know exactly what she was doing with Vasco every night.

She'd said "No, thank you," to the more flirty dresses with low-cut cleavage and plunging backs, and picked a rather demure ice-blue satin dress that fell to her ankles. It draped flatteringly over her curves but didn't reveal too much. Why give them more to gossip about?

"You look beautiful." Vasco's warm breath on her neck made her jump. She stood at the top of the stairs looking down into the foyer, as a well-dressed crowd of visitors trickled in, removing velvet capes and even furs despite the warm fall temperatures. All of the women were stunning, including the older ones, and dressed with the elaborate elegance of people who took seeing and being seen seriously.

"I'm a little nervous." Her palms were sweating and she didn't dare wipe them on her delicate dress.

"Don't be. Everyone's thrilled to meet you."

"Do they know, about Nicky and you and…"

"Only that you're my guest of honor." He kissed her hand, which made the tiny hairs on her skin stand on end. If only this were all over and she could lie in his arms in "their" bed.

She wasn't sure whether to be relieved that the guests didn't know the truth or worried that this meant they could therefore guess and speculate in all directions.

Vasco slid his arm into hers and guided her down the stairs. His proprietary touch silently introduced her as his girlfriend. The bright, winning stares of richly dressed females raked her skin like sharp nails and their tinkling laughter hurt her ears. Still she made her best effort at conversation—people spoke in English most of the time, presumably for her benefit—and managed to keep a smile plastered on her face.

Vasco looked devastatingly handsome in black tie. Somehow he made even the formal dinner jacket look rakish and daring. He touched her whenever they were near, just a brush of his knuckles along her hip, or a dusting of fingers over her wrist. Each time it made her heart leap into her mouth and her skin tingle with awareness.

Hushed voices, especially in Spanish or Catalan, made Stella's face heat. She knew they were wondering and whispering. Did they think her too plain and ordinary for Vasco? Did they suspect a "compelling reason" of some sort to explain his interest in her?

"What brings you to Montmajor?" asked a woman about her age, with short dark hair swept into a glossy updo and a curious expression on her carefully made-up face.

"The library." Stella smiled as sweetly as possible. "I'm a book restorer and the chance to work with these ancient volumes is a dream come true." Ha. Didn't even have to fib.

The woman smoothed an imaginary wrinkle out of her black lace dress. "Are you enjoying our local hotel?"

Stella swallowed. "Actually it's easier for me to stay here at the palace. Closer to the library." She cleared her throat.

"Of course it is." A slim eyebrow arched upward. "Such a lovely building. With so many bedrooms." Her voice dropped slightly for the last phrase. "I've seen some of them myself." Her dark eyes sparkled a challenge.

"Really?" Stella tried to sound amused. "Are you one of Vasco's old girlfriends?"

A crease appeared between the carefully plucked eyebrows. "Vasco and I are very old friends, but he could never claim I was simply his girlfriend." She said the word as if it tasted nasty.

Stella felt herself shrink a couple of inches. She'd been so pleased and proud to have Vasco call her his girlfriend. "Oh, you were just lovers, then?" She couldn't believe how bold she was being.

And it backfired again.

"Yes." The woman glanced across the room, and

her eyes darkened. Stella ventured a guess that she was looking right at Vasco. "Lovers." A lascivious grin crept across her reddened lips. "That's exactly what we are."

The use of the present tense dried Stella's response on her tongue. She took a hasty swig of champagne.

"Have I embarrassed you?" The velvety voice seemed to mock her. "I am accused of being blunt sometimes. But nothing embarrasses Vasco, I assure you."

She turned and walked away, leaving Stella staring, openmouthed. This woman obviously considered herself to be Vasco's current lover. Or one of them, at least. Maybe she was housed in some other well-appointed room at the palace. A square turret, perhaps, or an octagon.

She glanced around, looking for Vasco, and spotted him laughing with a bubbly redhead, whose pale breasts practically poured out of her red bustier. Now, that was what a royal mistress should look like.

Stella glanced down at her frosty-colored ensemble. Maybe she would have been better off with more *va-va-voom* so these women might see her as competition. She hated the pointy little spears of jealousy that pricked her as he took the woman's hand and kissed it, just as he'd done with hers earlier that evening.

Vasco was a charmer. A ladies' man. He couldn't help flirting and teasing and seducing women. Which made him utterly unsuited to any kind of lasting relationship.

A rather chinless young man asked her to dance and she accepted, glad of the opportunity to keep busy. They chatted about books and the local language and culture in his halting English while he whirled her around the floor to a brisk waltz. Stella inadvertently looked at Vasco a couple of times, but was never gratified by him staring jealously back. He seemed to be enjoying himself and had probably forgotten she was there.

After midnight and the end of a multicourse buffet dinner she was tempted to sneak upstairs on the pretext of checking on Nicky and not come back. As she slipped out a side door of the ballroom into a quiet corridor, a hand on her arm made her jump.

"I've missed you tonight." Vasco's eyes glittered. "I prefer being alone with you."

"Me, too," she said honestly.

"Let's go to our room."

Her whole body said yes. In the privacy of the round chamber, Vasco peeled off her dress and devoured her with a ravenous gaze that made her feel like the most gorgeous woman on earth. He feasted on her with his tongue and she enjoyed caressing and tasting his whole body. A banquet much more tempting and satisfying than the one downstairs.

By the time they finally made love she was so aroused she thought she'd climax immediately, but Vasco made a meal of delaying and slowing his movements, taking her right to the brink, then pulling back, until she was almost hysterical with passion. They climaxed together then lay breathless and happy in each other's arms.

No one else mattered. How could they? When she was alone with Vasco everything was perfect.

But when she woke up later in the night he'd gone. Did he go back to join the party? Possibly even to share his advanced lovemaking skills with another woman? She'd left her son in the care of a sitter night after night for a man who claimed they were a family but offered no permanent commitment.

Sooner or later riding this emotional roller coaster was going to catch up with her.

Vasco returned to the party feeling a buzz that didn't come from the vintage Montmajor wines they enjoyed. Time with Stella always left him feeling refreshed and glowing with good cheer.

"Hey, Vasco." His old friend Tomy called to him from near the bar. "I thought we'd lost you for a while there."

"I had some urgent business." He took a glass of champagne from a waiter.

"I noticed. The American girl seems to have quite a hold on you." Tomy raised a blond brow.

"She does indeed." He sipped the bubbly liquid, which only echoed the fizzing of arousal that still pumped through his system. "She's the mother of my son."

Tomy's eyes widened. "So the rumors are true."

"Every word of them. Little Nicky has brought life to the palace and so much joy to all of us."

"Why didn't any of us know about him?"

"It's complicated. I didn't know about the boy until recently. I'm having to move carefully and take my time."

"You will marry her, won't you?" Tomy looked skeptical even as he asked the question.

Vasco's muscles tightened. "You know the Montoya men aren't cut out for marriage."

"That's never stopped them before. You know the people of Montmajor will expect it of you."

"I've spent my life defying expectations and I don't plan to stop now. I have no wish to marry anyone."

"What does the girl think about this?"

Vasco frowned. "We haven't discussed it. Like I said, it's early days, and she's a freethinking American who values her independence. She's not looking for a man to marry."

They hadn't discussed it, mostly because despite the intimate tie of Nicky, they were just getting to know each other. How many people started discussing marriage after a month? Usually people dated for years before committing these days. She probably didn't know what she wanted yet any better than he did.

Tomy's lips curved into a smile. "So you intend to keep her here as some kind of concubine?"

"No!" He took a swig of his champagne. "Of course not."

"A lover, then."

Vasco took in his friend's amused expression. "Yes, a lover. Why not?"

"Because women are never satisfied with simply being a lover. Maybe it won't happen this week, or this month, or even this year, but sooner or later she'll want some kind of commitment from you, in the form of a ring. Especially since there's a child involved."

"I'll keep her happy." He'd found that a kiss soon dissolved any tension or confusion that arose between him and Stella.

Tomy gave him a wry smile. "For a while you will, then she'll want to marry you."

"A fate to be avoided at all costs." Vasco glanced around at the crowded room. At five in the morning the party was still going strong. "Marriage ruins all good relationships. How many of the married couples in this room don't despise each other? They all go out to parties so they can dance and flirt with other people. The wedding day is when a relationship starts a perilous downhill journey to hatred and resentment."

"Your parents were married for more than forty years."

"And despised each other for every second of it. They only married because my dad was forced into it when she became pregnant with my brother. They may have even loved each other once but there was no evidence of that during my childhood."

"Your father did like to share his affections."

Vasco snorted. "With every woman in Montmajor. My mother only put up with it because she hated scandal and drama."

Tomy shrugged. "That's how it goes. You marry the pretty mother, then continue to enjoy extracurricular activities. No need for the fun to end because you find a queen. Have your cake and eat it too, as the Americans say."

Vasco shuddered. "No, thanks. Too much cake will rot your teeth and clog your arteries. There are some Montoya traditions I mean to break with."

"We noticed when we saw your proclamation making relations legal between unmarried couples." Tomy grinned. "Very romantic."

"There's no reason to make the mother of my child a criminal."

"You're such a sweet guy." Tomy shoved him playfully. "No wonder every woman in Western Europe has the hots for you. You do know all the other girls will take your unmarried status to be an open invitation."

"If I got married they'd just see it as an intriguing

challenge." Vasco raised a brow. "I think I'm safer single."

Tomy shook his head. "If only I was you."

The ball, with its large and gossipy guest list, set rumors buzzing round Europe. Stella found herself drawn to the websites of paparazzi rags which linked her name with Vasco's and speculated openly about Nicky.

It was humiliating to know that people all over the world could ooh and ahh and guess over their romance—and she didn't know any more about where it was headed than they did.

"You're taking it too seriously," protested Karen, when she phoned her late one night. She knew Vasco would be waiting for her in "their room" and she hated herself for being so eager to head there. "Let loose and enjoy yourself."

"Trust me, I have been. That's half the problem. If I had any discipline I'd confront him and ask him where this is going."

"Why don't you just let things take their own course?"

"I'm trying." She sighed. "But I have a feeling we'll carry on like this forever."

Karen laughed. "What's wrong with that? It sounds like you're having a fabulous time."

"I came here to Montmajor so Vasco could get to know his son. I've done everything his way and I've even discovered that I love it here. But I can't stay here, sleeping with him every night, as some kind of live-in girlfriend."

"Why not? Sounds perfect to me."

Stella stretched herself out on the bed in her own room. "I guess I'm not cut out for prolonged dating. I must be old-fashioned. Remember how I was always trying to get Trevor to go one step further?"

"That's because you wanted kids."

"Yes, but I also wanted to get engaged, and married. Does that make me strange?"

"No, it makes you boringly normal. Don't be boringly normal. Seize life by the horns and Vasco by the...well, whichever bit sticks out most."

"You're horrible. I don't know why I even called you." She couldn't help smiling as she let her head rest on the pillows. "And of course that's exactly what I'll go do the moment I hang up this phone."

"Thank goodness. I'd hate to think of him going to waste. I saw the pics of you on the *Hello* website and he's seriously droolworthy."

"You're looking at those websites, too?"

"Human interest. Those of us who don't have a life of our own live vicariously through the exploits of lucky ladies like you."

"All I wanted was to quietly raise my son and restore books."

"Now you're doing both of those and sleeping with the hottest guy in Europe. Oh, and he's a king. I'm crying into my coffee for you."

"Be serious. I have to decide whether to stay here with Nicky, or bring him back to the States. Vasco wants me to stay, but I've already decided that I can't live here as his lover indefinitely. It's not fair to me or to Nicky. We've been here a month and I'm sure it's starting to feel like home to Nicky. I need to know whether it will be our permanent home, or if I'm just another in a long line of girlfriends."

"A month isn't a very long time."

"It's been long enough for me…" *To fall in love.* She didn't want to say it out loud. Right now it was just her secret.

A month might not be much in a conventional relationship where you meet the person for a date once or twice a week, but they were living together and saw each other all day long, not to mention all night long. Well, except those lonely early mornings. It was a fast-forward kind of relationship, and in the public eye, too. If total strangers wondered and gossiped about where they were headed, she'd be foolish not to want some concrete answers, too.

"What, you're bored with him as a boy toy already?"

"I wish."

"Uh-oh. I think I get it now. You're getting in deeper than you imagined and you want to know whether to go all the way or pull back while you can still save yourself."

"You have amazing insight. I've never felt like this about anyone, including Trevor." Not even close. "And I know from my years of living on this planet that this kind of relationship ends in marriage or tears."

"Or both."

"Thanks for your support." Stella rolled over. Vasco would wonder where she was if she didn't leave soon. Maybe she should keep him guessing for a change, so he wouldn't take her for granted.

"Just ask him."

Stella laughed. "You make it sound so easy. Hey,

Vasco, will we be getting married or are you saving yourself for someone hotter?"

"Leave out the last part and you'll be fine. Or ask him to marry you."

Stella sucked in a breath. She could never do that. The prospect of rejection was far too agonizing. But there was another possibility. "Maybe I could ask him if he intends for Nicky to be his heir. If he doesn't marry me, then Nicky doesn't inherit. At least not if Vasco has another child."

"Go for it. That could be a good deciding factor on whether you stay. Does Nicky seem happy there?"

"Very. He's gone from being shy and almost nonverbal to the most babbling and outgoing little boy. I think he loves being doted on by caring relatives rather than competing with lots of little go-getters in day care. The slower pace of life here works nicely for him."

"And for you."

She hesitated. "I do love it here. It's a bit like living in a five-star hotel all the time. The people are so lovely and I have work most restorers could only dream of."

"And Vasco."

"For now."

"Go ask him." Karen sounded firm. "Just find out what's in his mind. And don't call me back until you do!"

The abrupt dial tone sent a frisson of anxiety through Stella. She peeled herself off the bed and slipped her feet into her shoes. Vasco would be waiting for her with that warm, seductive smile on his sensual mouth and a twinkle of mischief in his eyes. She had to get her question—whatever it might be—out before she fell under the spell of his touch and his kiss and all sensible thought retreated into oblivion.

She passed one of the porters in the hallway and nodded a greeting. She wasn't even too embarrassed anymore about running into people on her nightly perambulations. Surely everyone in the palace knew what went on between her and Vasco. No doubt they accepted it as a normal and natural part of life in a royal house.

With a royal mistress.

She didn't feel like a "girlfriend," whatever that was. She lived in his palace and ate his food and wore designer clothes he paid for. Girlfriends took care of their own rent and phone bills and went out for nights on the town with their other friends. She was a kept woman right now, even if she did have a job that paid far more than the going rate.

"El meu amor." Vasco's deep voice greeted her from the darkness of the round chamber. *My love.* Did he feel the same way she did?

She closed the door behind her and searched for Vasco's moonlit outline on the four-poster bed. Silver rays picked out his muscled torso and proud, handsome face. He lay naked on the covers, arms outstretched to welcome her. "Come here, I'll undress you."

She steeled herself against a desire to climb right into his embrace and surrender herself. "I've been here a month." Better spit it out before she succumbed. "I want to know where Nicky and I stand. Long-term, I mean."

"You live here and it's your home."

Her heart beat faster and her courage started to fail

her. Did she want to risk losing what they had? "I can't be your girlfriend forever."

"You're far more than that."

"I know, I'm the mother of your son, but what does that mean for us in the future?" She straightened her shoulders. "Will we marry? Will Nicky be king one day?"

He laughed. "Already looking ahead to when I'm dead and gone?"

"No." The word shot out. How rude she seemed with her demands. "No, not at all." The prospect of Vasco dying was unimaginable. A more vital and indestructible man would be hard to find. "It's just that…I want us to be a real family and…"

Her words trailed off. *I want us to live happily ever after.* Her face heated and she was grateful for the darkness. There, she'd said it. Put all her pathetic hopes and dreams out into the dark air, where they now hung in silence that stung her ears.

"Stella." He rose off the bed and moved toward her. "We are partners in every way."

She braced herself as he came close. The warm masculine scent of him drifted into her nostrils, taunting her. "I don't want to be a royal mistress. People are talking. All the papers are speculating. It's embarrassing."

"People always talk and write about members of the royal family. It's just part of life in the public eye. There's no need to read that stuff or trouble yourself with it. Our life is ours alone and no one else matters."

He slid a powerful arm around her waist and her belly shuddered in response. Why did he always sound so sensible and make her feel she was being silly?

She tried to picture the worst-case scenario. "Do you plan to marry someone else one day? Another aristocrat perhaps?"

Vasco's throaty laugh filled her ears. "Never. Never, never, never. Our son will be king and you will always be my queen." He pressed his lips to hers and a flash of desire scattered her thoughts. "Let's enjoy tonight."

His hand covered her breast through her thin blouse. Her nipple thickened under his palm and her head tilted back to meet his kiss. How did he always do this to her? Already her hands roamed over the warm, thick muscle of his chest. Again she was intoxicated by the sheer pleasure of the moment.

Maybe she wanted too much. Couldn't it be enough to enjoy life here in this lovely place with a man she was crazy about? Vasco undressed her slowly, working over her body with his tongue. She arched her back, letting herself slide into the ocean of pleasure he created around her. Most women would kill for a lover this sensitive and creative, let alone all the other things she enjoyed in the palace.

She ran her fingertips over the hard line of his jaw, enjoying the slight stubble that roughened his skin. Vasco's eyes gleamed with desire as he looked up at her while sliding her pants off. The chemistry between them was undeniable. She'd never felt anything like it. Would she seriously walk away from Vasco because he didn't plan to marry her?

Her whole body shouted "No!" Vasco took her in his arms and they rolled on the bed together, wrapped up in each other. Her body craved his and judging from his arousal and the soft words he breathed in her ear, the feeling was mutual.

She exhaled with relief as he entered her, and they moved together in a dance of erotic joy that swept them both up into their own world of bliss, where no one else existed. Afterward, she was too tired to think, let alone speak.

But she phoned Karen the next day, as promised.

"He said I'll always be his queen." It sounded pretty promising when you said it out loud like that.

"What more could you want?"

"A wedding date. You remember how Trevor always put me off with excuses and reasons for delay. All that *We're too young. We have our whole lives ahead of us. You can't rush these things.* Maybe he even meant it at first, but he got comfortable with the way things were and decided not the change them."

"Vasco's not Trevor, thank goodness."

"If there's one thing I've learned in the last decade, it's that a man who's determined to dig his feet in can stand like that forever. After we broke up, Trevor got more honest and admitted that he'd never have married me or had a child. He didn't want the responsibility."

"I always told you he was a creep."

"He's comfortable living in a pleasant limbo between carefree boyhood and the responsibilities of family life. He wanted the reassurance of knowing he had a date on Friday, but not the commitment of diapers to change or college fees to pay."

"Or a wife to still cherish and adore when she had silver hair and crow's-feet." Karen chimed in. "He's like my ex. They like to keep the escape clause open."

"I can't live like that. Not anymore. I decided that when I broke up with him and made the choice to start a family by myself. I chose a life on my own terms and embraced it, and I'm not going to turn around and live life on someone else's terms that I don't agree with, and that's what I'm doing right now."

"One month, Stella. It's not exactly the same as nine years."

"That nine years happened one month at a time, because I just kept waiting. Never again. It's worse now because people I don't even know are curious. You should see the headlines—'Royal wife or royal mistress?' It's totally humiliating."

Karen sighed. "I think I could get used to being a royal mistress, if there were enough diamonds involved."

"Oh, stop."

"But I have a crazy idea."

"Knowing you it really will be crazy."

"Listen, if you asked him whether you're getting married and he fobbed you off with some fluff about being his queen, then maybe you can call his bluff."

"How so?" Already a nasty sense of misgiving writhed in her gut.

"If you told one of those gossip rags that you and Vasco were getting married, would he deny it?"

Stella shrugged. "Probably not. He'd just nod and smile and say 'one day' or something like that."

"But what would he do if you told them you definitely weren't getting married?" Her voice had a calculating tone.

"You've lost me."

"He's used to running his life the way he wants it and having everyone follow along nicely. If you, the mother of his child and heir and the woman he sees as his queen, says she won't marry him, he's bound to protest, right? Men always want what they can't have. It's reverse psychology."

"Well…" Karen had a point. He probably would be upset by an outright refusal.

"And he'll want to prove you wrong."

"By proposing and making me his wife within the week?" She laughed, but the idea was oddly intriguing. "I don't know, Karen. It's not my style."

"You've tried your style and it's not working. If he won't discuss your future with you in private, flush him out in the open. At least then you'll get your answer one way or the other. If you really want it, that is."

Stella bit her lip. "You're right. If he's not going to marry me I'd rather know now, so I can move on with my life. Your idea is crazy, but it just might work."

Nine

Getting the information to the press was easy. Stella had figured out that the "mystery" gossip editor of the local paper was a rather glamorous older widow who lived on an estate near the town. Anything she printed had a way of getting out into the mainstream media, too. Probably because she couldn't resist telling everyone she knew when she found a piece of actual gossip.

Since this woman, Mimi Reyauld, was constantly fishing for new items, she would be easy to leak it to. After only three expeditions to the local town for magazines or a new toy for Nicky, Stella managed to "run into" her in the market square.

"Stella, my dear, don't you look lovely?" Mimi had a bouffant blond 'do that didn't move in the wind. "How is that gorgeous boy of yours?"

"Nicky's having his afternoon nap. It's a great time for me to come stretch my legs and do some shopping."

Mimi's gaze raked her hand. "He's such a dear. I'm sure he'll be the spitting image of his father one day."

Stella smiled. She hadn't openly acknowledged Nicky as Vasco's, but she knew people assumed he was. Clearly Mimi was fishing. "I'm sure he will. Are you coming to the masked ball on Friday?" Almost every adult in Montmajor was invited to the legendary annual festivities and the palace was abuzz with preparations.

"I wouldn't miss it for anything. Vasco throws such wonderful parties." She leaned in and her expensive scent stung Stella's nostrils. "When will we be celebrating your engagement?"

"Engagement?" Fear made her pulse skitter and she pushed back her hair with her ringless hand. "Vasco and I have no plans to be married." So far she'd said nothing but the honest and sad truth.

Mimi's eyes widened. "Come now, dear. Don't be modest. Everyone in Montmajor can see the two of you are madly in love."

Stella's tongue dried. They could? How embarrassing. She knew it was true for her, if not for Vasco. "I'm not sure where they're getting that idea. Vasco and I won't be getting married." It hurt to say it out loud, but if that was going to be the truth, better to find out now rather than months, or years, down the road when it would be harder to extricate herself from the awkward situation.

"Oh." Mimi's mouth formed a red circle of surprise. No doubt she'd been hoping to be the first with the engagement scoop because she looked disappointed.

"I imagine there will be a lot of other ladies who'll be happy to hear that." She hoisted her chic little bag higher on her shoulder. "And I look forward to seeing you at the ball, though I dare you to try to recognize me in my mask." Mimi air kissed and walked away, leaving Stella feeling a little stunned.

She'd done it. Other things she'd mentioned to Mimi even in passing had almost invariably shown up in print—there just wasn't that much good gossip in Montmajor—so it was inevitable this latest tidbit would, too. It seemed very European to have the local gossip columnist be an old friend of the family.

That night with Vasco she felt like a traitor. He hadn't sworn her to secrecy about their relationship but she'd been very discreet until now, not telling anyone except Karen what was—or wasn't—going on. Even his inviting embrace and his spine-tingling kisses didn't entirely banish the sense of guilt she felt for talking about their relationship in public.

The next morning, sure enough, the story had made it into the gossip column, and by the afternoon it had spread like wildfire through the European tabloids, culminating in headlines like "Dashing Vasco Montoya Still Europe's Most Eligible Bachelor."

It didn't take long until Vasco noticed.

"What's the meaning of this?" He brandished the local paper. "You told Mimi we're not getting married."

"Mimi?" She played innocent. "What does she have to do with the local paper?"

"She's Senyora Rivel, the gossip columnist. Everyone in Montmajor knows that."

"And you still invite her to the palace?"

"She's a sweet old lady who never writes anything harmful. But why did you say this?" His eyes flashed. She'd never seen him look so serious. Not exactly angry, but...annoyed.

Part of her was excited and grateful that he cared. "It's the truth. We're not getting married."

"Says who?" He strode toward her.

"We've made no plans. Every time I ask you about the future you start kissing me or change the subject." She couldn't believe how bold she was being. She'd never be capable of it if Nicky's future wasn't at stake, too. "Since apparently everyone else is talking about our marriage plans, I thought I'd better start setting them straight."

Confusion furrowed his noble brow. "I think our relationship should be between us, and not anyone else's business."

"I didn't make a proclamation, I just had a short chat with Mimi at the market. Since it's the truth, there's no harm done."

His eyes narrowed slightly. "Now everyone will want to know why we're not getting married."

Her heart contracted. He'd now confirmed what she said. Part of her wanted to die right now on the spot, or sink into the stone floor. She managed to keep a straight face. At least now she knew where she really stood.

"Then tell them the truth." She swallowed hard. "Tell them we're not in love." She held her breath, while her chest ached with hope and despair and she silently begged him to argue with her and say that he loved her with all his heart and soul.

But he didn't. He simply stared at her for one long, searing moment, then turned and sauntered away.

Crushed, Stella shrank against the nearest wall as she heard his footsteps recede into the distance. She'd hoped her little media revelation would be the catalyst that would draw them together. Instead it had just the opposite effect. At least she had an elaborate silver-sequined mask to hide her tears behind at the ball that night.

Vasco, masked like everyone else, stood amidst the flow of arriving guests. Anonymity added a certain feverish excitement to the occasion, and champagne flowed like a summer rainstorm. Anger still thudded through him like distant thunder. He'd been surprised by how much Stella's words wounded him.

He hadn't held up a magnifying glass to his feelings for Stella, but they were intricate and involving. She'd come here as the mother of his son but transformed into far more. Their nights together wove a web of passion that bound them tightly, even when Nicky was asleep on the other side of the castle. He loved her company and craved it when he was busy working or held up with other tasks.

Stella had quickly become the center of his existence and he shared his life with her in the most intimate way imaginable. Only to have her coldly deny their relationship in public.

There was no denying that he'd pushed back a little when she'd asked about the future. They'd known each other a short while and the future was a very long time. There'd be plenty of time to make decisions about that later. He'd been overwhelmed by the new emotions crowding him since he learned about Nicky, let alone his feelings for Stella. He needed time to adjust to the reality that his family had expanded and these new people were now closer to him than his own parents or siblings had been.

Then she came right out and said that they didn't love

each other? Something unfamiliar and painful gnawed at his gut.

He took a swig of his champagne and listened for the strains of music flowing over the crowds from the adjoining ballroom.

"Cavaller." A female masked in shimmering green sequins greeted him in the old style.

"At your service, madame." He kissed her hand, which was soft and scented, but not Stella's.

He knew exactly where Stella was right now. Standing on the far side of the room in a blue dress and matching mask. He'd determined to ignore her all night—shame he couldn't take his eyes off her.

The hurt and fury raging in his blood made him almost want her to flirt with another man so he could be angry and call her a tease and despise her for cheating on him. But so far she'd spoken only to women and men over the age of seventy.

"Your masked ball is a sensation, as always." The lady in green had a deep, seductive voice that he didn't quite recognize.

"You're too kind. Would you honor me with a dance?"

Her dark eyes glittered behind her mask. "I'd be delighted."

He slid his arm through hers and risked a glance at Stella to see if she'd noticed. Irritation rippled through him that she was deep in conversation with one of the town's elderly librarians and not paying any attention to him.

He tightened his arm around the waist of his companion's green silk dress and guided her to the dance floor. He gave the band's conductor the cue for a tango, and led her into the middle of the crowd as the first sultry strains swept through the room. He didn't need Stella. He'd always enjoyed a full and exciting life and there was nothing to stop him continuing that. Stella had as much as given him permission.

He twirled his partner and dipped her, and she flowed with the movements like hot butter, a smile curving on her red-painted mouth. Another lightning-fast glance at Stella revealed that she was watching him.

Ha. He pressed his partner against him and executed several quick steps and another turn that made her dress sweep around him. His muscles hummed with the sheer joy of movement. Another glance confirmed that Stella's eyes were still fixed on them, and he fought a triumphant smile. She might not love him, but she was certainly paying attention.

After the dance his green-masked partner gratefully accepted a glass of champagne and offered to remove her mask and reveal her face.

"Don't take off your mask," he murmured. "Tonight is for mysteries and magic."

"But I know who you are," she protested. "Doesn't it seem fair that you should know who I am?"

"Perhaps life isn't supposed to be fair."

"I suppose that's a good attitude for a king. Not everyone can inherit a nation." She hesitated and leaned closer. "Is it true that you've already sired an heir?"

"It is." He'd never deny Nicky.

"Then you've chosen your bride, as well." Her eyes shone with curiosity.

"Who knows what the future will bring." He picked up her hand and kissed it. His intention was to taunt Stella, though he managed to resist glancing at her to see if she was watching. He could feel her gaze on him like a touch.

Even if she didn't love him, Stella was deeply attracted to him and he'd be sure to stoke the fire of her passion when they were alone later tonight. In the meantime, apparently flirting and dancing with other women was an excellent aid to focusing her attention.

"Hello." A statuesque girl in silver with a long fall of blond hair and a pouting mouth touched his arm. "What a wonderful party."

He turned readily away from Ms. Green. "I'm pleased you're enjoying yourself."

"Very much so." Her eyes lit up inside her mask. "And I've always wanted to meet you. I'm—" She had a French accent.

He pressed a finger to her lips. "Don't spoil the enigma. Let's dance." He didn't want to know who she was. He took her hand and led her into the crowd of dancers, where he whirled around with her, losing himself in the pleasure of the dance. Stella was only one woman in a world of millions.

So why was she the only one he wanted?

Stella shrank further into the shadows each time she saw Vasco smile at another woman, or kiss her hand. At first she couldn't take her eyes off him when he danced. He moved with muscular grace and the skill of a professional dancer. Women seemed to melt into his embrace, and their besotted smiles dazzled her like car headlights when she made the mistake of looking at them.

Did she really think she could be his one and only? Even if she hadn't infuriated him with her little press leak, he'd still be dancing and flirting with other girls in his role as host. Women flocked to him like iron filings to a magnet. He wasn't just rich and royal, he was gorgeous and mischievous and charming and obviously enjoyed their company. No wonder he didn't want to marry her. Why would he give up all this to spend his life with her?

Far too much to hope for. She was an ordinary book restorer from an ordinary suburb who lived a quiet, humdrum and happy existence until Vasco swept into it like the Santa Ana winds and made her realize how much she'd been missing until now.

Thank goodness for the mask. It was hot and itchy but at least it hid her expression of despair. She'd been shamefully lax about looking for jobs—too busy enjoying her work here—and had barely kept in touch with anyone because she didn't want to reveal too much about her situation. Maybe she just couldn't bear to think about leaving.

And there was Nicky. Instead of being gone eight hours at a stretch with him in day care, she could spend time with him every hour or two when she took a break, and in the meantime he received individual attention from people who adored him. They'd even arranged for some staff to bring their young children to the palace so he had playmates to laugh and sail his boat with. His vocabulary had gone from less than five words to full sentences in both English and Catalan, and his joy in his daily existence was undeniable. No more tears as she left him at day care, or endless colds that he picked up from the other kids.

Could she pull him from this peaceful existence that

suited him perfectly and drop him back into their old hectic routine again? If she could even find a job.

A waiter offered her champagne and she shook her head. She needed to keep it clear as both of their lives depended on the decisions she'd make now.

She didn't relish the idea of Nicky being king, but it didn't seem like such a hard life either, if things did work out that way. And if they didn't, because Vasco married another woman...

Fierce jealousy twisted her insides. It was physically painful to watch him laughing and talking with other girls, let alone marrying them and having children. At least if she went back to the States she wouldn't have to see him and be tormented by what she wanted but couldn't have. She knew Vasco had no legal rights to claim Nicky or even see him again. If she chose to, she could leave here tonight with her son and never look back.

The prospect made her cold. She knew in her heart she could never do that to Nicky, or to Vasco. Now that the father she hadn't intended for her son to have had manifested himself in their lives, she could see how much Nicky adored and looked up to him. Vasco himself had opened his home to them with such generosity and goodwill, and had thrown himself wholeheartedly into the role of father. In all honesty that was one of the reasons she'd fallen so hard in love with him, and she'd rather die than take his son away from him.

So she and Nicky had to stay.

A furtive glance across the crowded room found Vasco in the arms of yet another woman. Tall and wrapped in a slinky purple dress, her white mask flashing bright as her smile. Stella grimaced beneath her own festive disguise. She'd have to tell him that from now on they could no longer be intimate. She'd be an employee, like all the others, not his lover. She wasn't cut out to be a royal mistress and she should know by now that she'd never be anything else if she stayed here.

Clutching her sadness like a cloak about her, she slipped out of the room and into a quiet corridor. Vasco wouldn't even notice she was gone. He hadn't said a word to her since the party began. No doubt he wanted to put an end to any rumors about them being involved, let alone married.

She pulled off her mask, climbed up to her room and peered into Nicky's adjoining one where tonight's sitter, one of the palace cleaning staff, sat in a chair reading a thriller. "You can head off for the night. I'll be here." She managed a shaky smile.

"Are you sure? I don't mind staying until morning." The young girl looked a little bashful. Everyone in the palace knew that all-night sitters were the order of the day because Stella spent her nights in the round tower with Vasco.

But no more. "No thanks, I'll be here."

She washed her face and put on the cotton pajamas she hadn't worn in as long as she could remember. The bed felt cold as she climbed into it. She'd grown so used to having a warm body next to her that the sheets seemed empty and uninviting without one.

She'd get used to it. She hugged her arms around herself and tried not to picture Vasco downstairs dancing with beautiful masked women. Would he take another of them to the round tower tonight? Or would he expect her to meet him there regardless of their argument?

Rolling over, she pulled the covers over her head to block out the strains of music that crept into the room from the party. She'd managed just fine without Vasco for most of her life, and she'd be fine without him for the rest of it. Maybe she'd even find another man, a more sensible and reliable and ordinary guy with whom she could have a real relationship. Kings weren't really cut out for modern relationships. They too readily expected everyone to be at their beck and call, and she'd certainly obliged so far.

Though after Vasco it could prove very challenging to find anyone else appealing.

She tossed and turned, listening over the faint music for Nicky's sleeping sounds, but she couldn't hear anything. He'd been in bed for hours and was a solid sleeper, so she couldn't even distract herself by humming lullabies or stroking him to sleep. She needed someone to hum her lullabies, but clearly she'd have to make do without.

There was usually a half-finished novel next to her bed for her to dip into at moments like this, but she hadn't slept here for so long that she'd neglected to find one. She could sneak off to the library and bring back something to read—not all the books were ancient manuscripts—but then she'd run the risk of encountering party guests in her pajamas. Or worse, seeing Vasco creeping off to some turret with his mistress-of-the-minute.

No. She'd have to tough it out here in bed. She'd resolved to stare at the dark ceiling until she either fell asleep or passed out, when she heard the door open.

"Who's there?" She sat up in a panic. Hadn't she locked it?

"You didn't come to our room." Vasco's deep voice penetrated the darkness.

Her chest tightened. He'd really expected her to go there after they argued and stayed apart all evening? "I thought I'd better sleep here."

"You're angry with me."

Was that was he wanted? A jealous rage to gratify his male ego? "No, just sleepy." She didn't want him to know how upset she'd been by seeing him with those other women. She didn't even know why. He hadn't done anything but dance with them. She certainly didn't want to give him the satisfaction of letting him know she cared.

"Me too. It's been a tiring night."

The room was too dark for her to see more than his outline, but she heard the sliding sounds of clothing being removed. She held her breath. Did he intend to come climb into her bed without an invitation? Her skin tingled under her cotton pajamas.

She heard something hit the floor—his pants? Her heartbeat quickened and she scanned the darkness. His warm, masculine presence moved through the room toward her. She clutched the covers.

"You can't just come get in bed with me." Her voice sounded shrill, like she was trying to convince herself.

"Why not?"

"I came here to be alone."

"Every time I danced with someone, I was thinking about you." His soft voice crept through the darkness and caressed her. "I pretended I was holding you, moving with you. The masks made it a little easier, but nothing compares with the real thing."

She bit her lip in the dark. Already her muscles softened, forgiving him everything, wanting him close. When she felt his weight tip the mattress, she couldn't bring herself to push him away. Then the covers lifted and he slid underneath. His thighs were warm, rough with hair, and his arms wrapped around her before she could summon the energy to resist. How arrogant of him to assume he'd be welcome! Yet the scent of him disturbed her senses and sent lust sizzling through her.

"You need to take these off." His fingers plucked at the buttons of her PJs. What if she didn't want to take them off? Maybe she did want to sleep?

Her body said otherwise. Already her muscles relaxed and her nipples tightened into peaks. Vasco slid her top off and kissed her firmly on the mouth before licking each nipple with his tongue. Passion stirred deep inside her and she found her hands clutching at his muscle and drawing him closer. Hard and ready, his erection only intensified her arousal.

He'd danced with all those other women, but it was her he came looking for in the darkness, to spend the night with. Her heart sang at the truth of it, and their kisses filled her with feverish hope and joy.

I love you. She wanted to say it but common sense prevented her. Vasco feared commitment—that was obvious—so he might be scared off by declarations of undying love. Still, what wouldn't she give to hear it from him?

He entered her slowly, kissing her with measured passion. His movements were restrained, slow, his hips barely shifting and his hands holding her still, so that she could feel every beat of both their hearts and feel each breath that filled their lungs. They lay there, suspended in time, senses fully engaged and aroused, bodies moving as one. Her anger and hurt had evaporated, replaced by joy and excitement that stirred her body and mind.

Her demand for marriage felt foolish now. What did some official piece of paper matter when it was so obvious they were meant to be together? Vasco didn't have to tell her in mere words that he loved her. She could feel it in his touch, in a language much more subtle and ancient than any of the ones she'd learned to speak.

They started to move again, this time with a fevered energy that made her gasp and shiver with desire. They rolled together on the bed, taking turns driving each other to new heights of arousal and intense emotion. The music from downstairs now seemed an accompaniment to their erotic dance, a celebration of their private passion. None of those people downstairs mattered anymore, just the two of them, traveling further and further out onto a peninsula of bliss.

Her climax swept over her in a cool shiver of ecstasy, and she felt Vasco explode inside her, gripping her with force and murmuring her name over and over again.

I love you. Again the words hovered behind her lips, but she didn't need to say it. She'd told him with her body, as he'd told her. There was no mistaking the connection that joined them. They shared a child, but more they shared something less tangible but just as precious in its own way.

"I missed you tonight." His whispered confession made her smile.

"I missed you, too. I thought you were mad at me."

"I was. Mad at you, mad about you." He kissed her lips softly. "I wanted to make you jealous."

"It worked. I wanted to dance with you."

She gasped as Vasco's strong arms whipped her out of bed and onto her feet. The cool stone shocked her soles, but his arms wrapped around her like a blanket as he guided her into a dance in the dark bedroom. Music still swirled in through the doors and windows, caressing them with its delicate notes. A strong partner, Vasco pressed her against him as he moved across the floor of the large bedroom, whirling her round and round, so light on his feet they might be floating.

With her chest pressed against his, naked and still warm from lovemaking, she followed his motion effortlessly. Eyes closed, she imagined them gliding through the crowds, then through the clouds, a perfect partnership.

"Whatever you wish, my lady." He twirled her one last time, then pulled up her hand to kiss it.

"Except marriage." The words flew out before she could stop them. Immediately she wished she could inhale them back inside her.

Vasco stiffened, still holding her. She felt him draw away, even though he didn't move. She'd broken the spell that held them together with her petty worldly concerns. "You should be glad. You've made it clear that we won't be getting married." His voice was quiet.

She was tempted to say she'd only done it in the hopes that he'd change his mind, but that would just make her look pathetic. If Vasco wanted to marry her, it would just happen. He was like that, a thunderstorm in motion. She'd been swept along on its high winds and pierced by its lightning bolts enough to know that. How else had she ended up living here in a strange country within weeks—days, really—of meeting him?

Now he did pull back a little, putting a couple of inches of darkness between them. "I'd like to formalize my relationship with Nicky. I want to be his true father in the eyes of the law."

Her chest tightened. "I don't imagine that will be too hard since you can change the laws anytime you feel like it."

She could swear she saw his smile gleam, despite the lack of light. It must be quite something to have that much power. Tempting to abuse it. She knew Vasco wasn't a cruel man, but he could be arrogant and demanding. No doubt that came with the territory of being king.

"I think a simple declaration will suffice. And perhaps a law confirming that children born out of wedlock can inherit the throne." He sounded thoughtful.

"I suppose that's just keeping up with the times." He wouldn't even need her consent. The DNA tests had confirmed that he was Nicky's father. She wouldn't try to take Nicky away from him now. Her son adored his tireless and playful father.

"Indeed. And it ensures that one day Nicky will be king."

They weren't even touching now. Their bodies had slipped away from each other, and goose bumps rose on her skin in the night air coming in through the open window. Perhaps it was simply his love for Nicky that brought him to her? Maybe he wanted to make sure she'd stay and this was the only way he knew how. He paid for her loyalty—and for his son's presence in his life—with passion that fired her heart but left his cold.

An ache of despair and loneliness crept over her, extinguishing the joy she'd felt only moments earlier. She turned away from him and climbed back into the bed. "We'd both better get some sleep." He must be anxious to slip away, as he did every night, back to his own realm. Away from her.

She heard him don his clothes in the darkness, even his mask, because she saw the sequins that edged it shimmer in the pale moonbeams that crept around the curtains. "Good night, Stella. Sleep well."

His kiss made her lips hum, and she hated the way her heart squeezed at his touch.

Of course now she wouldn't be able to sleep at all. Not that she could earlier. Being around Vasco was driving her crazy. One minute she was drifting on a tide of joy, sure that she was the happiest woman alive. The next she was alone and filled with anguish, sure that he didn't love her and never would. She could make all the plans and conditions she liked when she was alone, but as soon as she was in Vasco's presence all common sense and resolve evaporated in the heat of passion.

There was no way she could stay here in the palace with him and remain sane.

Ten

The local librarian put her in touch with some owners of nearby private libraries who might want a restorer. She didn't mention that she was also looking to live in. She struck gold with a nearby family who spent most of the year in Paris but had a small estate in Montmajor only a ten-minute drive from the palace. After a phone call and a reference from her old boss in California, they hired her to restore some rare volumes over the next three months. Most importantly, she could live in their villa, which would buy her time to find somewhere permanent to move and give her space to think about her life.

She waited a few days until Vasco went out of town. She knew that if she tried to confront him he'd just wear her down, probably with nothing more than a meaningful look. She'd tried too many times to stand up to him and failed more miserably each time. She needed to make her break when he wasn't there to cajole her out of her decision.

While she waited for him to leave she slept in her own bedroom, alone, with the convenient excuse that it was "that time of the month." She'd felt a mix of relief and disappointment at the realization that she wasn't carrying another of Vasco's babies. And her monthly visitor was welcome protection. If she slept in Vasco's arms at night, she'd lose every last ounce of conviction.

With no possessions other than those in her suitcase, the move required no planning beyond packing some of Nicky's toys into a box and calling a taxi.

"What do you mean, you're leaving?" Aunt Lilli's eyes widened with alarm. Her arms reached for Nicky, who ran immediately into them.

"I'm only moving up the road, to Castell Blanc. I'll be working in their library and living in the house. If you agree, and if Vasco is okay with it, I'd like to bring Nicky here every day to spend time with you."

"Vasco's not going to like this." Aunt Frida pursed her lips and shook her head. "Not at all."

Stella swallowed. "I know, but's too difficult for me to live here. It complicates matters."

"How is it complicated? Vasco is crazy about you." Aunt Mari crossed her arms. "You must marry him."

Stella blinked. "He's made it clear that he won't marry me. Or anyone else, I think. He doesn't like the idea of marriage and said it ruins relationships."

"But you're the one who told Mimi you'd never marry him."

"Only because I knew his opinion already. To be honest I was hoping he'd see it differently, but he's as determined as ever to remain single and I can't live here as some kind of…" She glanced around, then lowered her voice. "Concubine."

Lilli sucked in a breath. "I've had words with him. I've tried to explain to him that you're a nice girl." She hesitated.

Stella pondered that if she was such a nice girl she wouldn't be in a position to be called his mistress.

"He's stubborn," Lilli continued. "Obstinate."

"A typical man," cut in Aunt Frida.

"Perhaps you moving out is for the best. He'll realize what he's missing."

Stella shrugged. She wasn't going to get carried away hoping things would change. People rarely changed. "I want Nicky to grow up with his family, including all of you. I intend for us to stay here in Montmajor, but I need to leave the palace right now, today."

Lilli nodded. "I understand." Still, she looked very sad as she stroked Nicky's cheek. "You'll bring him tomorrow?"

"Without fail. Unless Vasco barricades the castle against me."

"He's not that foolish." Aunt Mari looked down at Nicky. "I do hope he'll see sense before it's too late."

Her feet and her heart felt heavier than her suitcase as she walked through the grand archway out of the palace. Silly, as she hadn't come here to marry him. She also hadn't planned to fall madly in love with him. That was the real reason she had to go. It was just too painful to fall asleep in his arms dreaming of them as a real family, knowing all the while he saw her only as his girlfriend—enjoyable and potentially disposable—and that he had no plans to ever commit to a permanent relationship.

Heck, he wasn't even there when she woke up in the morning!

Maybe if she hadn't waited nine years for a commitment from Trevor—which never came—she'd feel differently, but her life had made her who she was, and she'd sworn she'd never let anyone do that to her again.

"What do you mean she's gone?" Vasco scanned the hallway behind Aunt Lilli. He'd returned from his short trip to Switzerland midday on Sunday, and the palace was eerily silent.

"She moved out four days ago." Lilli pursed her mouth in that disapproving way he remembered from his childhood. "She said it was a personal matter." She raised her brow on the word *personal*. No doubt she didn't want to reveal too many details in front of the staff.

"Come to my study." He strode past her. How could Stella do this? She was happy here in the palace, he knew it.

Though she had been avoiding him for the last week. Her excuse about having her period was convincing at the time but now he grew skeptical. She'd known all along that she was leaving and she wanted to keep her distance.

He flung open the door of his office and ushered Lilli in, then slammed it again. "Nicky, where is he?"

"He's with Stella, of course."

He blew out a curse. "She said she'd stay here. That she liked Montmajor and she knew it was a good place for Nicky to grow up."

"She hasn't left the country. She's living at Castell Blanc."

"Oscar Mayoral's old place? Why is she there?"

"She's working on books in the library. And living there."

"How does she even know Mayoral?"

Lilli shrugged.

At least the landowner was in his seventies. And married, with several children and grandchildren, so there was no immediate risk of losing Stella to him. "Doesn't he live abroad?"

"Yes."

He frowned. "So she's there alone?"

"There's a housekeeper, a handyman and a gardener."

He inhaled and tried to wrap his mind around Stella living anywhere other than right here in the palace. It felt wrong. "I must bring her back home."

"She no longer wishes to live here as your...lover." His elderly "aunt" narrowed her eyes slightly as she said the last word.

"She told you that?"

"In so many words. She knows you won't marry her and she's too principled a lady to live here in sin with you, especially with her son to consider."

Vasco snorted. "Live in sin? Not everyone has the same outdated moral code as my aunts."

Lilli lifted her pointed chin and crossed her arms. "No. They don't." Her gaze accused him. She clearly felt that he was at fault. "She wants to marry you."

"She told the press she'd never marry me."

His "aunt" clucked. "Nonsense. She told Mimi she knew *you'd* never marry her. That may not be how she phrased it but we all know it's the truth." She walked up to him and adjusted his collar, which made him feel like a naughty schoolboy again. "And she won't live here anymore unless you marry her."

Something deep in Vasco's gut recoiled from the implied ultimatum. "Marriage is not for me."

Lilli shook her head and clucked her tongue in that infuriating way of hers. "Then apparently Stella is not for you, either. Or Nicky."

Panic flashed through him for a second, then he calmed. "She agreed to let me become Nicky's legal parent. He'll officially be next in line to the throne."

His aunt snorted. "After you're dead? How consoling. Don't you want to enjoy him in your life right now?"

"Of course I do." Why did Stella have to mess things up when they were going so well? "Are you trying to say that Stella won't let me see Nicky unless I marry her?"

"Stella brings Nicky here in the mornings during the week to spend the day with us. She has no intention of keeping Nicky away. Just herself."

He frowned. "So she'll still be coming to the palace." He'd see her every day. He could tempt her. He'd already proved that.

"I know what you're thinking, young man. If you try to seduce her you'll only drive her further away. Stop thinking like a lover and start thinking like a father."

Vasco wheeled away. That's exactly what he didn't want to do. If he started planning his love life around domestic practicalities, it would end up as loveless and unromantic as his ancestors'. Passion and duty just didn't go together.

"Do you love her?" Lilli's quiet question penetrated

his thoughts and almost made a sweat break out on his brow.

"What kind of question is that to ask a king?"

"Don't make light of it. It's a question you need to ask yourself."

"I don't know what love is. I'm a Montoya man, remember?"

She snorted. "That's the trouble with you. Montoya men keep their brains in their breeches, that's why they've relied on women to keep this good country going all these years."

"I should have you thrown in the dungeons for such a treasonous statement."

She raised a stern penciled brow, but humor twinkled in her eyes. "I can see I'm making you think."

"Nonsense. You're making me annoyed. And hungry. Do they not serve lunch around here anymore?" He needed to end this conversation. "Please ask Joseph to serve it immediately." He turned away and pulled out his phone to signal that the conversation was over.

His aunt Lilli didn't budge. Barely more than five feet tall, she seemed to occupy the entire space of his office with her willful presence. "Bring her back home, Vasco. For all of us."

"Ms. Greco, there's someone very important here to see you." The elderly caretaker wiped her hands anxiously on her flowered housedress. Her wide eyes said it all.

"His majesty." Stella managed not to look up from the large letter *E* she was touching up on a seventeenth-century bible. It was Sunday and she was trying to squeeze some work in during Nicky's afternoon nap.

"Yes. He's at the door right now. Which room should I bring him into?"

Stella swallowed and put down her tiny paintbrush, sure she wouldn't be able to keep her hand steady enough not to destroy the precious book. She would have loved to say, "Send him away!" but that would have scandalized and horrified the housekeeper, and wasn't fair.

"I'll come to the door."

"I can't leave him standing there." Already the old lady was shocked.

"I'll go right now." She closed up her bottle of ink. The most important thing was not to weaken and fall into his arms. Not that he'd want her to. If he thought chatting with a gossip columnist about her lack of marriage prospects was a breach of trust, then moving out had probably set his hair on fire.

She hurried past the flushed housekeeper and headed for the front door. The housekeeper's gnarled husband, who was the live-in handyman, hovered hidden behind an archway.

"The king!" he sputtered, as she went by. Apparently they hadn't been reading the gossip columns or they might have expected his majesty to show up. Castell Blanc was a very quiet place. She'd been here four days—since Vasco left for his trip—and no one had visited at all, not even a Jehovah's Witness. Now suddenly the local monarch was cooling his heels on the doorstep.

She managed to prevent a hysterical giggle from rising to her throat. It was late afternoon and warm amber light brightened the foyer and poured through the half-open door. She could see Vasco silhouetted against it, standing just inside the doorway.

"What does this mean?" His deep voice greeted her before she could even see his face.

"Let's go outside."

"No, I'd like to come in."

"It's not my house so that's not appropriate." Her heart beat like a freight train. She didn't want the elderly couple to hear their conversation. He might be king but that didn't mean he could just march in anywhere like it was his own palace.

She walked past him, avoiding his glance, and out the front door. Unfortunately his spicy masculine scent tickled her nostrils as she passed, and sent darts of misgiving prickling through her.

He followed her down the wide steps. Castell Blanc was a large house, maybe three hundred years old, built of mellow golden stone. It had the air of a summer residence, not well updated or overly maintained, which suited its rustic charm. She hadn't even met the owner. He'd hired her over the phone on the strength of her Pacific College references and her acquaintance with a respected local librarian, who was too discreet to mention her circumstances. What would Senyor Mayoral think if he knew his new book restorer was angering royalty on his front doorstep?

A vast paved courtyard, surrounded by disused stable buildings, sprawled in front of the house.

"You're not going to let me in?" He looked both amused and astonished. Vasco had probably never been denied entry anywhere. She'd even let him into her L.A. house eventually.

"I can't."

"I'm sure Oscar wouldn't mind."

"I came here to get away from you." She felt indignant that he didn't even seem to be listening to her. "I need some space."

"There's plenty of space at the palace. You could have your own wing."

She felt the urge to growl. "And you'd be able to saunter into it whenever you pleased. That's what I'm trying to get away from."

Why did he have to be even more handsome and good-humored than she remembered? He looked striking and quite unroyal in jeans and a dark green shirt. The thin layer of dust suggested he'd arrived on his motorbike, which was just so…Vasco. It was hard to be mad at him in the flesh.

Which, of course, was the whole reason she needed distance between her flesh and his. "I don't want a relationship where I'm at your beck and call but there's no permanent commitment between us. You may find that bizarre, especially since we haven't been together very long, but that's just how I feel. I've been there already with my ex, and it's not for me. I'm sorry, but I can't do it again."

"Your ex and I are totally different people."

"On the surface, this is true. On the other hand, you're both men and neither of you wanted to commit, so maybe you have more in common than you think."

"This is all about marriage, for you?" He frowned.

She inhaled a breath. "That makes it sound like I'm making an ultimatum, but I guess it is about marriage, when you come right down to it. If I choose to be in a relationship, then it's because I am seeking the kind of lifetime partnership that I think all of us deserve.

I'm not a teenager looking to experiment, or a college student interested in playing the field. I'm a mature woman and the mother of a young child. At this point in my life I either want a committed relationship, or I'd rather be single."

She'd made that decision when she told Trevor she wouldn't be available on Friday nights anymore. No more dating "just for fun." Once she realized a relationship wasn't going anywhere, she wanted out. Which was probably why she hadn't taken a chance on one since. Was she a freak because she wanted a committed, loving relationship?

"We can be committed without being married." Vasco's gray gaze implored her. "Marriage doesn't work out well for the Montoyas."

Again desire warred with fierce irritation. Why did his eyes have such an infuriating sparkle to them? "You aren't your ancestors, you're you. We can't just live together in our situation. You're a king. We have a child. No one knows the true details but right now I have 'live-in royal mistress' stamped on my forehead like a supermarket chicken. Nell Gwynn may have been happy with that arrangement, as long as Charles II gave her enough money and houses, but I'm more old-fashioned and can't live like that."

She glanced around, suddenly worried the elderly caretakers might be listening. "I don't want people talking about me. About us."

"But they will anyway, because Nicky is our child."

"They don't know the truth about his conception." An idea made her stand up straight. "Maybe we should tell them? We're not lovers at all, simply strangers brought together by the freezers of a California sperm bank."

Vasco shivered. "No."

"Why not? It's the truth. You made the choice to leave your deposit there. It's not like you didn't know what you were doing."

"I wasn't the king then, and didn't think I ever would be."

"I don't see the difference." She tilted her head. "You made the generous act of donating your DNA—for a small fee—and I made the choice to buy it. Why does it matter if you're the king or just some bored teenager with a grudge against his family."

"Because as king my children inherit the throne of Montmajor."

"As you've pointed out, that can happen anyway. Wave your magic wand and change whatever laws you need to." Speaking to him like this was liberating. Now that they were out of the castle—his domain—she felt freer and able to be irreverent and argumentative in a way that she couldn't while she was his guest.

"If people knew they'd be shocked."

"So shock them." She smiled sweetly. "I never intended to conceal the truth when I made a choice to use a sperm bank. I don't think it's any different than adopting, you're just doing it at an earlier stage of life."

"You're saying I put my sperm up for adoption?" Vasco squinted in the sun.

"Exactly. Nothing embarrassing about it."

He snorted. "I'm ashamed of doing it. I was young and stupid."

"But if you hadn't done it, Nicky wouldn't exist."

"True, and I'll always be grateful for him, but…" He turned and stared into the distance for a moment.

"But you'd rather have people think he was conceived during a moment of breathless passion." She narrowed her eyes.

His dimples reappeared and that infuriating twinkle lit his eyes. "Exactly." He walked toward her, and she crossed her arms and braced herself against the appeal of his outstretched hands.

"How come there isn't a male word for *mistress?* It doesn't seem fair that I get to be the naughty one in everyone's eyes. I could tell the papers you're my royal boy toy."

He laughed. "Go right ahead. Happy to oblige. Now if you'll just invite me inside…" He stepped closer, until his warm, intoxicating scent crept into her nose.

"No, thanks. I have books to restore."

"Including the ones at my library. Surely you haven't abandoned your duties?"

"I'd be happy to continue my work once relations between us are settled." Ack. That sounded like another ultimatum. At least she knew he'd never agree to anything just to get his books restored. He wasn't that much of a bibliophile. Still this whole situation was mortifying.

"My aunts told me you'll bring Nicky to spend the day with them." His gaze softened. He looked almost apprehensive, if such a thing was possible.

"I will. I have. I don't want to take Nicky away from you. That's why I'm still in Montmajor. I can see that this is his home and he loves it here."

"And you?" Again, his eyes shone with something different from their usual mischievous sparkle.

"I love it here, too." Her heart ached.

I love you, too. But he knew that already. It didn't matter. He knew she'd drop everything and rush back to the palace to marry him if he offered. But he didn't want that.

"So you're staying." He shifted his weight, arms hanging by his sides, but with tension in them as if he wanted to reach out and hold her there.

"I'm staying, but on my own terms. If I'm going to live here I'll have to build a life that suits me. I've been a guest in your house for long enough. Lovely as it is, it's not my home."

"Nor is Castell Blanc." He gestured at the big house behind her.

"No, but it's a good place to stay while I figure out my long-term plan. I need to settle in and assess my employment prospects and what kind of house I can afford."

Vasco laughed. "You have the coffers of Montmajor at your disposal and you're worried about finding a job?"

She wrapped her arms around herself. "My independence is important to me. I don't want to be a kept woman."

He frowned. It was clear he had trouble understanding her point of view at all, which was exactly why she needed to keep distance between them. She suspected that under his thoughtful exterior he was just waiting for another opportunity to seduce her back to his lotus-eating isle of pleasure where she didn't care about the future but only the blissful present.

Which would undoubtedly happen if she let him get too close.

"Stella." He said her name softly. His gaze rested on hers for a long moment that made her breathing shallow. She had the feeling he was about to say something powerful and important. Maybe he would ask her to marry him? Her heart quickened and she felt blood rise to her face.

How quickly that would solve everything. She could accept his offer and return right home with him. Oscar Mayoral wouldn't mind very much if his books didn't get restored, at least not right away. They'd been in the same condition for at least two hundred years, so what was another year or two?

Vasco still hadn't said anything. Emotion passed over his face, deepening a tiny groove between his brows. His mouth twitched slightly, which reminded her of how it felt pressed to hers. Her palms heated, itching to reach out and hold him.

"Come home with me now." He stepped toward her until she could almost feel his body heat through her clothes. How easy it would have been to say yes.

But she stepped back. "Have you not been listening to me at all?" Tears hovered at the edges of her voice. "Next you'll come out and issue a law that I have to come live with you at the palace. You can't have things all your own way. I've been very obliging so far, in moving across the world with my son—who is probably standing in his crib wondering where I am right now—and settling into a brand-new country and culture. But I have my limits. You can't just seduce me into fitting into your life on your terms twenty-four hours a day. I'm staying here and that's final."

Why did he not look more shocked? He seemed almost amused, as if he was contemplating her idea of enacting a law to keep her at his side. Anger fired her mind and body. "If you try any sneaky moves I'll tell the press how Nicky was conceived."

She watched his Adam's apple move as he swallowed. "I'll respect your wishes." *For now.* The unspoken words hung between them. Vasco was not used to having his plans thwarted. She had a feeling he'd be back with some new scheme to wrap her up in his palace cocoon and keep her and Nicky there on his terms.

She'd have to be strong.

Which was so hard when she wanted nothing more than to run into Vasco's warm embrace.

"Please leave. I need to check on Nicky and you can't come in. I'll bring him to the palace on Monday as usual." She turned away, feeling rude and cruel even though she knew he deserved it.

She half expected to hear his footsteps behind her on the courtyard, but he didn't move. Suddenly chilly, she ran up the steps and in through the door. She didn't stop running until she got to Nicky's bright bedroom on the second floor, to see him still peacefully asleep in the antique crib.

"Oh, Nicky." Unable to resist, she picked him up and squeezed him. He snuffled and rubbed his eyes, not quite ready to wake up. "You're the only man in my life who matters." She held him close, his big head heavy on her shoulder, and his warm, sweet-smelling body filling her arms and soothing the tension in her limbs.

He was the reason she couldn't stay at the palace as Vasco's concubine. He was too young to understand now, but in only two or three years he'd know about moms and dads and marriages. She was well prepared to be a single mom. That she'd planned for and eagerly anticipated. But when her son asked why she and Daddy weren't married, she wanted to be able to answer truthfully, and say it simply wasn't meant to be, rather than still be sleeping in Vasco's bed and hoping and praying that one day he'd finally ask her to be his bride.

She was cured of that kind of false hope. If a man wanted to marry a woman he came out and asked her. If he didn't…well, then the woman moved on, no matter how hard it was to make that break.

Eleven

"So you admit I was right." Still astride his Yamaha, Tomy pulled off his helmet.

"About what?" Vasco removed his own helmet. Hot and sweaty, he didn't feel any more relaxed after burning fuel up and down the Pyrenees all day.

"That your lady would want a ring on her finger."

"You're supposed to be taking my mind off the situation." He shot his friend a scowl. The sun was high in the sky, scouring both them and the mountaintops with harsh light. Tomy's blond hair stuck up in spikes.

"How does that help? The situation is still there when you go home."

"I wish it was. I told you Stella moved out." Just saying it out loud made him feel hollow inside. The palace seemed like the loneliest place on earth since she'd been gone.

"Are you just going to give up on her?"

Every nerve in Vasco's body recoiled with a snap. "No way!"

Tomy laughed. "You are in love."

"I have no idea what love is." It couldn't be this painful ache that haunted him every time he thought of Stella.

"Sure you do. It's like the feeling you have for your Kawasaki." He gestured at Vasco's dark blue bike, which was covered in a thick layer of dust.

"I have three of these. And two Hondas and a Suzuki."

"Okay, then the feeling you have for Montmajor."

"That's pride, and passion. And a whole bunch of stuff that's probably twisted into my DNA. Not love."

"Hmm." Tomy's mouth twisted with amusement. "Methinks he doth protest too much."

"Lust, I know all about. That's a powerful emotion." It stirred inside him right now, as he let Stella's face drift into his imagination. He wanted nothing more than to hold her in his arms, kiss her…

"Lust is a sensation, not an emotion, so if you're feeling it in your heart, it's probably love."

His heart just plain hurt. And talking about it made it worse. Usually he could count on Tomy to distract him from serious matters. "Are we really having this conversation?" He wiped a grimy sleeve across his face to mop up the sweat. "Because if we are I think some alien has seized my friend's body and is holding him hostage somewhere."

"Entirely possible." Tomy glanced down at his big hand, sprinkled with pale hairs. "I hope the alien chicks are having fun with me."

Vasco snorted. "See? What do you know about love? You're with a different girl every time I see you."

"And I love each and every one of them." Tomy smiled and stared at the horizon. "Especially Felicia. I'm seeing her tonight."

"You're a bad influence."

"I know. You shouldn't associate with me." Tomy drew a heart in the dust on his engine casing. "Something's different since you met Stella."

"Since I learned about Nicky, you mean." Was that when everything changed? His life hadn't been the same since he laid eyes on his son.

"That too. Stella and Nicky come as a package, but I can tell it's not just the kid you're crazy about."

Vasco inhaled a long, deep draught of mountain air. Shame the air was hot, and somewhat smoky from a nearby fire. "Stella's an amazing woman. She's bright and funny and gorgeous. I love that she restores books and that she was prepared to do anything to fulfill her dream of having a child."

"So marry her."

"Marriage is the death of fun. Suddenly we'll be bickering about palace protocol or what to have for dinner and everything will seem like a chore."

"Says who? I can't see you arguing with anyone about palace protocol."

"This is an observation. Not just of my parents but other married couples both of their generation and ours. Once you marry, the relationship becomes a job."

"They're not you, Vasco. Even your job is play. Look at you, for crying out loud." He gestured at Vasco seated on his bike high on a sunny hilltop. "You're not only king of a small nation but you have a large stone mining company with offices on several continents. You manage to turn any work into play."

"Or maybe I've figured out how to keep work where it belongs and play where it belongs." That's what he'd always told himself. Why didn't it seem a satisfying answer anymore?

"Is that why you don't ever have women in your bedroom?"

"I told you that?"

Tomy nodded. "You want to be able to skip off at a moment's notice."

"Exactly. See? Stella is better off without me." Why hadn't he invited her into his own room when he had the chance? Now his attempt to keep his life ordered and compartmentalized seemed petty and foolish.

"You might find you like waking up with her."

Vasco shoved a hand through his damp hair. It certainly was hell spending all night alone and waking up without her. "I might." Right now nothing seemed more appealing than the prospect of waking to Stella's sweet face.

"So marry her."

"But I know marriage will ruin everything."

Tomy laughed, then shook his head. "Vasco, my friend, you've already ruined everything. She's moved out and taken your son with her. How much worse can it get?"

"Good point."

"Besides, you're a king. If it doesn't work out you can always lock her up in a tower and have some fresh maidens delivered." Tomy's eyes twinkled.

Vasco's muscles tightened. This was no laughing matter. "If I wasn't sitting on a bike I'd…"

"What?" Tomy climbed back astride his own bike. "How about you race me down to the river instead."

Adrenaline surged through his veins. "You're on."

Vasco had paced the halls all night trying to decide if he should marry Stella. Whenever he decided "yes," it felt strange and frightening—not feelings he had much acquaintance with.

Whenever he decided "no," it felt wrong. The prospect of spending the next few decades without Stella in his bed, or at his dining room table, or by his side made his soul rattle.

Which meant he should do it.

But would she even say yes? He was pretty sure she had wanted to marry him. She'd even said as much. She was attracted to him, she seemed to like him a lot, and he was Nicky's father.

On the other hand, he'd done enough wrong to drive her out of the palace and he'd come right out and said that he didn't believe in marriage. Not very confidence-inspiring words for a potential fiancé.

The prospect of her rejection made him realize how much he desperately wanted her to say yes. Just think, she could be back in the palace by tomorrow night, with his ring on her finger and a smile on her lovely face as she climbed into his bed.

In his bedroom.

He marched through the palace, heels thundering over the stone. Dawn was just beginning to throw daggers of light onto the vast array of weapons in the armaments hall when he came up with his plan. He paused in front of the ornate armor that had recently encased Stella's lovely body. Stella loved pageantry, all the old medieval stories of knights and maidens. He'd get dressed up as a knight and ride over to Castell Blanc, where he'd serenade her and ask for her hand.

How could she resist that?

There was no sign of Vasco that morning when Stella dropped Nicky off at the palace. Her son looked so happy to be back in the loving arms of his aunts, who had planned a picnic for him and a playdate with two children from the village. Still, she felt a little empty leaving the palace without even seeing him.

He must be angry that she wouldn't come back and slot into the routine he'd planned, especially after her threat that she'd reveal the truth about how Nicky was conceived.

It was the truth, after all.

She left the palace feeling a little downcast, but determined to throw herself into her work and enjoy the sunny day. The car she drove belonged to Castell Blanc, and the owner had agreed to let her share it with the caretakers. It had turned out that neither of them could or would drive—they cycled into town for what minor supplies were needed—so it was hers alone. Everything was working out almost too well to be believed. She had a lovely, if temporary, home for her and Nicky, a job doing what she loved, and she could bring Nicky to see Vasco and his other relatives every day.

Yes, she felt a little empty inside, but that was just the wrench of leaving the only romantic relationship she'd ever really enjoyed, and because she didn't have any other friends here. She'd been so wrapped up in Vasco she hadn't bothered to make any. Now that she'd found her backbone and taken her life back, she resolved to join an evening class at the local school—there was one about Catalan poetry, and a series on sushi preparation—and get more settled into the local community. Sure, they might look at her strangely at first, but as long as she didn't confirm or deny anything they'd soon realize she was a person, not a tabloid headline.

She bought a baguette in the bakery and some of the local cheese, along with some olives and salami, and made herself a pleasant brunch on the terrace outside Castell Blanc. After a cup of coffee she settled into the enjoyable work of restitching the worn binding of an eighteenth-century book about the Roman conquest of Europe.

It had not been easy for Vasco to squeeze himself into the largest suit of armor in the palace. People were a lot smaller back then. There was no way the leg pieces would fit, but he managed to buckle the breast piece and arms on loosely and jam his feet into the crazy metal shoes. The big problems started when the horse saw him.

"Tinto, it's just me." He clanked over the cobbles toward the terrified beast. "Your ancestors would think nothing of this getup."

The pretty gray mare snorted and jerked her head up, eyes staring. The groom held tight to her bridle, but couldn't keep her feet still. Vasco propped up the visor, and looked at her. "I need you to work with me, Tinto. I have a maiden to woo."

The groom tried to disguise a grin.

"Once I get on her she'll be fine." He tried to reassure himself as much as the horse and her handler. Tinto herself was wearing fancy ceremonial tack, including an embroidered saddlecloth and tasseled reins. They'd make quite the romantic picture together—if he could just mount up.

He clanked a few steps closer, but the horse only skittered farther away across the stone courtyard. The groom tried to reason with her but she looked like she was about to turn and bolt for her field. Riding her would be interesting, under the circumstances. Still, he knew Stella would love it, and surely the armor functioned much like safety gear, right?

"Lead her to me while I stand still. Maybe that will work." He smiled reassuringly at the mare, who responded by snorting and pawing at the ground. Jaume, the groom, tried to lead her closer, but she planted her feet and peered suspiciously at him down the length of her proud nose. "Maybe give me some treats. Some of those mints she likes."

Jaume called out to Luis, who came running over with a fistful of candies and placed them awkwardly in Vasco's armored hand. Lucky the metal cased gloves were leather underneath and surprisingly flexible. He managed to get the wrapper off and place one on his other palm, then reach out his hand. "Here, Tinto. It's your favorite."

Tinto looked interested, but wary. She tossed her head and sent her white mane flying. After about a minute she took a hesitant step toward him, then another, and took the treat. "See, I knew you'd figure out it's me. You're part of a very important plan." He spoke softly to the mare. "Now we just have to figure out how to get me up on your back." He looked from his metal clad foot to the wide, ceremonial stirrup. This armor must weigh a good seventy-five pounds. It wouldn't be easy to get airborne. "Luis, could you give me a hand?"

Luis, who was neither young nor tall, shuffled over and wove his fingers together into a kind of human stirrup. Vasco knew he'd probably cripple the man if he stepped on his hand. "How about Luis holds Tinto and Jaume gives me a leg up." Jaume was young and strapping. A relieved Luis took hold of the reins and Jaume strode boldly over, in turn looking relieved not to be holding one thousand pounds of potentially explosive horse.

"One, two…" Tinto neatly sidestepped out of the way before Jaume could give him a leg up. "Oh, come on. No more mints until I'm up." He frowned meaningfully at the horse. "It's barely a fifteen-minute ride. You'll be home eating hay before you know it."

Luis maneuvered Tinto back into position. Lightning-fast, Jaume helped heave Vasco up into the saddle and he slung his leg over and came down as lightly as possible on Tinto's back. Tinto immediately wrenched free of Luis's grasp and took off bucking across the courtyard. "Easy!" Vasco grabbed the reins and tried to bend her neck to get control. He clanked and rattled like a bag of bolts as she skated over the cobblestones. "All right, we're off." He had the ring in his pocket. As long as that didn't fall out he was good.

He managed to steer her toward the gate that led from the stable yard out to the fields beyond, and all went surprisingly well until they got through the gate. Once they were outside the palace, Tinto threw in one more almighty buck, which pitched Vasco over her head. He landed on the ground with a loud series of clanks—and some very nasty sensations in his muscles—and managed to get his visor up in time to see her galloping off over the crest of the nearest hill.

He cursed. Luis and Jaume came running and helped him to his feet. The breast plate was dented and he felt pretty dinged, as well.

"You okay?"

"Still alive in here, I think. We need to catch her before she trips on the reins." He peeled off the armor and they spend most of the next hour following Tinto's trail until they caught up with her grazing quietly under an oak in a disused sheep pen. She had a small cut to one of her legs, so they led her back quietly and bandaged her up.

"Guess I'd better ride one of my other faithful steeds." He had enough bruises for one day. He changed into different clothes, this time a Chevalier costume he wore for parties sometimes. With the ring safely in the new pocket, he went and mounted his trusty Kawasaki. Not quite as romantic as a horse, but much more predictable. Within minutes he rode up to the entrance of Castell Blanc, propped his bike, and launched into song.

The roar of an engine made Stella look up from her sewing. It sounded like a motorcycle engine. Her heart started to rev and she put down her needle and moved to the window. The first strains of a male voice— singing—stopped her in her tracks.

Powerful and haunting, the raw music stole in through the open window and rooted her to the spot. Was it Vasco?

She stepped forward and peered gingerly outside. Her eyes widened as she looked down on Vasco dressed in embroidered silk breeches like a character from a

Cervantes story. Windswept and rugged as usual, and with his dark motorcycle only a few feet away, he looked impossibly masculine in the ornate costume.

But his voice… Deep and rich, it wrapped around the unfamiliar Catalan words and filled the air. Sound reverberated off the stone facade of the house and bounced back to the surrounding hills, growing and swelling around them.

"Oh, Vasco." She said it quietly, to herself. Just when she thought he couldn't be any more outrageous or adorable, he pulled some new stunt like this. Her heart squeezed and she wanted nothing more than to run into his arms.

Resisting that impulse, she had a sudden urge to show Nicky the fantastical vision of his father singing like an ancient troubador, then she remembered he was still at the palace with his aunts. Vasco was singing for her alone.

As she listened, she could make out a few of the words. Impassioned and heartfelt, the song seemed to tell of a heartbroken man who'd lost his true love and would never see her again. Tears almost rose in her eyes, not because of the lyrics, but because of the raw emotion in Vasco's melodious voice. Could he do everything? It didn't seem fair. How was anyone supposed to stand a chance around him?

He'd spotted her at the window, and even from the second floor she could see his eyes light up as he launched into another verse. Her own heart beat faster and excitement swelled in her chest. She soon found herself leaning out the casement window to fully enjoy the rapturous sound. Even a cappella, Vasco gave off more energy and intent than an entire orchestra of professional musicians.

And he was doing it all for her.

As a way to get into a woman's underwear, she had to recommend it. Right now she had chills and hot flashes going on at the same time. Still, she had to remain strong. This was about the rest of her life here, not some steamy afternoon scandalizing the housekeeper and her husband while their boss was away.

Tempting as that seemed.

Vasco reached the end of the song and made a dramatic bow and flourish. Stella clapped and couldn't help smiling. "Beautiful," she murmured, not even loud enough for him to hear.

"Would you do me the honor of coming to the door?" His courtly attitude amused and pleased her. Normally he'd just storm through the door without asking.

She nodded, and hurried away, pulse pounding. She dashed down the steps, telling herself over and over again to be strong. *Don't fall into his arms. Just say hello and tell him he's a good singer.*

"Hi," was the best she could manage, with a goofy grin, when she pulled open the front door to greet her dashing cavalier.

Vasco immediately got down on one knee and bowed his head. Stella froze. He reached into his pocket and fumbled for a moment, then pulled out a ring.

She almost fell down the steps. Surely he wasn't…?

He raised his head, and his gray eyes met hers with intensity that felt like a punch to the stomach. "Stella, I love you. I've thought about nothing but you since the moment I heard you were gone. I'm miserable without you and I know with agonizing certainty that I want to spend the rest of my life with you. Will you marry me?"

She stood rooted to the spot. Was she dreaming? She wanted to pinch herself but couldn't seem to move.

Vasco's gaze searched hers. She could swear she even saw a trace of anxiety cross his handsome face. He held out the ring a little farther. "Please Stella, be my wife."

"Yes." The word fled her lips without any permission from her brain. Why had she said that? His sudden change of heart was shocking and not entirely convincing. Still…

Vasco rose and slid the ring on her finger. The metal felt cool and sensual on her skin. He kissed her hand with deliberate passion, eyes closed. Then, face taut with emotion, he took her in his arms and pressed his lips to hers.

Her body went limp under the force of his kiss. If he weren't holding her close she'd have fallen to the ground. The whole situation was too amazing to be real.

When they finally pulled apart she looked down at his elaborate and historically accurate costume. Her doubts crowded back over her. "Is this a scene from a play that you're acting?"

"No, the words and emotions are entirely my own."

She frowned. "But yesterday you said…"

"Yesterday was an age ago. I had all night to contemplate the prospect of living without you and to realize how miserable I'd be if I lost you." His eyes shone with conviction that echoed deep inside her. "I've behaved like a spoiled child who wants to have everything his way, and ignore the feelings of others. Nicky needs a father who's a family man." He lifted his chin proudly.

Stella hesitated for a moment. "You're marrying me so that Nicky can have a proper family." An official marriage, without emotion. Something that looked good on paper, like all the Montmajor marriages before it. Her stomach tightened.

He took her hand, the one with the ring. "I said I love you and I mean it. You should know me well enough to understand that I'd never marry simply out of duty. I made it clear from the beginning that was out of the question." He paused and looked down for a moment, before his eyes fixed on hers with a penetrating stare. "It took some soul-searching to realize that what I feel for you has nothing to do with duty, or responsibilities, or anything else other than the joy I feel when I'm with you."

A strange warm sensation rose inside her. "I love you, too." It was a sweet release to let the truth out. "I think I've loved you almost from the start, when you showed up on my doorstep demanding a place in your son's life and unwilling to take no for an answer."

"Guess I'm lucky you didn't boot me out on my ear." He grinned.

"Well, I did try, but you're not easy to get rid of." She smiled, too. "And I'm glad of that, now." She glanced down at the ring. It was unusual, with an ornate tooled gold setting, and the stone was a bright blue sapphire rather than the more conventional diamond. "Is this an old ring from your family?"

Vasco faked a shudder. "No way. I don't want us following down their dreary path in marriage. I had it flown in from Barcelona overnight. Given your love of history I thought you might like something dramatic and historical looking, rather than an ordinary diamond solitaire like everyone else."

"You're so right. I adore it." The clear blue stone reflected the bright sky above.

"The stone was mined by my company in Madagascar, and I had it tooled by my favorite jeweler. I bet if you look closely enough you can see the whole universe in there."

She lifted the ring. It sparkled with astonishing brilliance and drew her eye to its depths. "I've never seen anything like it. I keep forgetting that you have a whole company out there in addition to being king."

"Comes in useful at times like this."

"And you're the type of person who needs to keep busy."

"Like yourself. I don't see you wanting to sit around all day staring out the window. Still, I do think you should be restoring the royal collection rather than a few tatty old novels here at Castell Blanc." His dimples showed as he made a dismissive gesture at the house behind her.

"Mr. Mayoral has a wonderful collection. Not as large as yours, of course, but every bit as distinguished in its own way." She smiled. "Still, I admit that I miss the lovely palace library. There isn't enough room for me to set up my tools in the library here so I have to bring the books into a spare bedroom."

Vasco looked pleased. "Perhaps you can bring his books to the palace to work on, if you still want to restore them."

"Maybe I will." Her muscles tingled with excitement at the thought of moving back to the beautiful palace with Nicky. It must be almost time to go pick him up.

Except that she didn't have to pick him up. The thought struck her hard and she glanced at her ring just to check again that she wasn't dreaming. "Are we really getting married?"

"You still don't believe me?" He stroked her chin, humor in his eyes.

"I want to, it's just a bit much for me."

"We're one hundred percent absolutely definitely getting married. As soon as possible. Today would be fine, in fact."

"Today?" She glanced down at her jeans and plain blue shirt.

"Or tomorrow. Or the next day. Or next month. I'll leave it entirely up to you. It depends on what kind of wedding you'd like to have. I vote for big and fancy with everyone we've ever met in attendance." His teeth gleamed as he smiled. "Just so they know we really mean it."

She laughed. "You know, you might have a point there. A big, fancy, over-the-top royal wedding with all the trimmings would give the paparazzi what they're looking for, and then maybe they'll leave us in peace."

"Never happen." He grinned.

"Oh, well. Maybe we should seize some peace right now." She glanced back at the house. A week and a half of abstinence from Vasco's lovemaking was catching up with her. His intoxicating male presence, especially in the dashing musketeer outfit, made her want to rip his clothes off right there. "Would you care to come inside?"

Her courtly invitation made him laugh. "I certainly would. I'm so glad I'm now permitted entry."

"We'd better not tell Mr. Mayoral about what we're about to do."

He raised a brow. "My lips are sealed. And I can't wait to find out what we are about to do."

Twelve

The carriage wheels rattled over the ancient cobbled streets as crowds cheered the wedding procession. Stella didn't need to worry about smiling for all the people watching. She'd had a grin plastered to her face all morning.

"I'm amazed the horses aren't spooked by all the helicopters." A fleet of them had hovered overhead since dawn, filming the wedding party as they emerged from the cathedral, and the long, colorful procession as it wound through the streets of Montmajor.

"They're used to them." Vasco beamed, as well. "Much less scary than a man in a suit of armor."

"Suits of armor seem to be a theme in our relationship." She murmured the words in his ear.

"So true. We'll have to get the horses acclimatized to them so we can try jousting." His arm rested around her waist and he pulled her closer. Arousal sizzled through her. How long would it be until they were alone again? The aunts had hovered over them all morning, and hairdressers and dressmakers had fussed and prodded and poked her until she was ready to scream. Now it was torture being right next to Vasco—in full view of the entire world.

Nicky sat opposite them in the carriage, with aunt Lilli holding tightly to the sash of his waistcoat to prevent him from jumping out into the throng. He even waved along with the grownups, and people called out "*Hola,* Nicky!" as he passed, much to his delight.

At last the carriage pulled up at the palace, where preparations were underway for the biggest party in Europe. Friends and family and thousands of diplomats and dignitaries had flown in from all over the world. Every room in the palace had been pressed into service as accommodation, and guests were billeted throughout the town.

A red carpet of rose petals covered the ground between where the carriage stopped and their entrance to the palace, and their sweet scent filled the air. A hundred white doves flapped and pecked around the petals and gravel and glided silently overhead. "Why don't they just fly away?" Stella whispered, as she alighted from the carriage and looked around her in awe.

"They prefer caviar on toast to grubbing for insects." Vasco grinned and waved to the assembled palace staff, who launched into some ancient Montmajorian greeting, half spoken, half sung. Vasco led her into the castle. Her lush ivory dress had a train nearly fifty feet long, and the six little train-bearers—boys of only seven or eight—rushed forward to gather and lift it behind her.

"I really do feel like a queen in this getup." She smiled at their serious expressions.

"You look like one." Vasco kissed her hand. "A coronet suits you." The tiny crown, tipped with rubies, was pinned to her elaborate hairstyle. If anyone had ever told her she'd wear an outfit this outrageous to any occasion, she'd have laughed, but the palace staff and wedding planners had snuck each detail in gradually until it was far too late to protest. Vasco simply laughed and said that if people enjoyed a bit of pomp and ceremony, why not give it to them?

Vasco himself was in a rather dashing getup that made him look like a nineteenth-century cavalryman. It even had tall shiny boots and acres of gold braid. His hair, of course, still looked windblown and wild, which only made him even more gorgeous. She could imagine women all over the world sighing and smiling as they looked at the pictures, and wishing they were her.

And who wouldn't?

Vasco lifted Nicky into his arms, and she squinted against the glare of flashbulbs. There seemed to be an insatiable appetite for pictures of Europe's most eligible bachelor as a family man. She hadn't told anyone that Nicky was conceived in a lab. It didn't seem relevant now they'd long since made up for the lack of sex during his conception.

Her skin tingled as Vasco took her hand and led her into the grand ballroom. A large glass fountain in the middle of the room bubbled with champagne. A waiter scooped two slender glasses of it for her and Vasco, and they turned to face the crowds—and yet more media—to raise a toast to their marriage.

"I'm the luckiest man in the world." Vasco lifted

his glass. "I live in the best country, I'm married to the kindest, loveliest woman and I have a wonderful son. Who could ask for more?"

Stella wanted to laugh. Even if they did ask for more, Vasco had that, too, starting with the fountain of champagne. The crowd cheered and the guests flocked around them with congratulations. Champagne poured late into the night and the guests enjoyed a feast of Montmajor specialties and hours of rousing traditional dances. By the time the guests finally trickled away to their beds, Stella was exhausted.

"I think you might have to carry me upstairs."

Vasco seemed tireless, as usual. "I'd be delighted."

"I may even have to actually sleep tonight." She raised a brow.

"Sleep?" Vasco whisked her off her feet. The train had been removed from her dress shortly after the toast, but she still wore about an acre of frothy taffeta that threatened to swallow him. "Sleep can be such a waste of time."

He lowered his lips to hers, and stirred a sudden rush of energy with his kiss. "Okay, maybe you have a point there," she gasped, when he finally pulled his mouth away. "I feel strangely invigorated." A funny thought occurred to her. "Wouldn't it be something if our second child was conceived on our wedding night?"

Vasco's eyes met hers, wide with surprise. "A second child?"

"Why not? Nicky would enjoy having a playmate." A tiny flame of fear licked inside her. Did he not want more children? They hadn't discussed it at all, and of course Vasco had never intended to have Nicky. Still, he seemed to enjoy fatherhood.

His expression turned thoughtful. Still holding her in his arms he strode for the stairs. He carried her into his old bedroom, which now truly was their room, and closed the door. They'd slept here since the night he proposed and brought her back to the castle. Her clothes had been moved into the large wardrobes that day, Nicky's things and child-safe bed were moved into one of the adjoining chambers, and there was no more talk of trysts in the round tower.

He laid her gently on the grand four-poster bed and tugged at the fastenings on her elegant dress. "You're so right. Tonight would be the perfect time to make Nicky's little brother or sister." A warm twinkle in his eyes warred with his serious expression. She wriggled slightly as he eased the bodice of her dress down past her waist.

She tugged at his cravat, then realized she needed to take out the gold pin that held it in place. It was hard removing all this crisp formal clothing when you were addled by lust and exhaustion. Probably in the old days they had servants standing around the bed to help.

"What are you laughing at?" Vasco's eyes crinkled into a smile.

"Just wondering if we'll get all these clothes off before dawn."

He pretended to tear at her fancy bra with his teeth. "We can always resort to scissors."

When she finally got his buttons undone she sighed at the sight of his hard, bronzed torso. Vasco really was hers, to have and to hold. Since she'd come back to the palace with the ring on her finger, their lovemaking had a whole new dimension. Gone were the nagging worries that she was making a huge mistake sleeping with her son's father.

And now they truly were married. She pressed her cheek to his chest, enjoying the strong beat of his heart. For a long time she thought she'd never know the joy of joining her life with another person. She'd achieved it in part when she had Nicky, but marrying Vasco made her life complete. They were a real family now, an inseparable unit. For the first time she could remember, she felt safe and protected, able to relax and enjoy the present without harboring doubts and fears about an uncertain future.

She gasped as Vasco pushed his fingers inside her delicate panties. Hot and wet, she shuddered against his touch. She'd never known her body could enjoy so many different sensations. There seemed to be no limit to the new feelings and emotions that crowded her mind since they became engaged. She could love Vasco, adore and enjoy him, without wondering what tomorrow would bring.

She wriggled under his sensual touch, suddenly aching to feel him inside her, to move with him and lose herself in the fevered intensity of the moment.

She reached for his erection and guided him in, and he let out a shuddering groan as he sank deep inside her. A wave of relief swept over her as it had every time since she'd come back. For those few brief but agonizing days at Castell Blanc she thought she'd never know this sensation again. She knew it would never be the same with anyone else after Vasco. He was a tornado that tore into her life and left it changed forever. Without him the aftermath would have been drab and lonely, but with him…

She arched her back and took him deeper still, then climbed over him and guided him into a fast rhythm. She felt no sense of self-consciousness making love with Vasco, just pure pleasure. He rose and fell with her, holding her close and kissing her face when she leaned forward, then flipping her under him and pinning her to the bed while he tormented her with his tongue and hands.

"Which would you prefer, a boy or a girl?" He whispered, at one intensely pleasurable moment.

Stella hugged him tight. "I don't care at all. I never did."

"I never even knew I wanted children." Vasco kissed her, holding her tight. "I didn't even think I wanted a wife. Thank heaven I found you."

They played in bed for hours, bringing each other to climax, pulling back, then starting over, in a rapturous exploration of their bodies and free-spirited baring of their souls. Somehow knowing that they could do this every night for the rest of their lives didn't diminish their hunger to enjoy each moment.

By the time dawn peeked in around the curtains they lay snoozing in each other's arms. "How long until we know if Nicky will have a new sibling soon?" Vasco's deep voice tickled her ear.

"About a month. It was an agonizing wait to find out if I was pregnant with him the first time. And the conception wasn't nearly as enjoyable."

"I'm not even going to ask how that happened, since I know I wasn't there in person." He stroked her cheek. "I should have been."

"We would never have met if it hadn't been for Westlake Cryobank." Stella grew thoughtful. "Instead of suing them for giving out my information I should send them flowers."

"Thank heavens for corruptible employees." Vasco grinned.

"You did pay someone off, didn't you?" They hadn't talked about it once. Somehow it was off-limits, too sensitive. Now that they were married, however, no topic seemed too touchy.

"Of course. Wouldn't you?"

She laughed. "No, probably not. But then I'm not a European monarch."

"Yes, you are." His steady gray gaze sparkled with humor.

Stella blinked. "You're right. How extremely weird."

"Queen Stella." He kissed her on the mouth. "Of Montmajor."

She shivered slightly. How strange. That's who she really was now. And her son—their son—was Prince Nicholas of Montmajor. It seemed a very dramatic title for a little boy who still loved to mash Cheerios with his fingers. "I suppose I'll get used to it eventually." She ran her fingers into his hair, then along his stubble-roughened cheekbone. "You've been married a whole day, almost. Is it as dreadful as you thought?"

His dimples appeared and he squeezed her with his strong, warm arms. "So far, so good. I think that since we broke with royal tradition by conceiving a child together before we even met, it's safe to say everything else will be different, and wonderful."

"I agree. And we'd better try to get a few minutes of sleep before our son wakes up."

Epilogue

One year and eight months later

"Blow, sweetie, blow!" Aunt Lilli held little Francesca up in front of her cake.

Stella laughed. "She doesn't understand. I bet she can extinguish the candles with her drool, though." She leaned forward to help blow out the single candle flickering amidst the shiny frosted decorations. They all sat around a big wooden table in the palace gardens, afternoon sun warming their glasses of fruit punch and sparkling over the silver cutlery.

Stella and Vasco had been thrilled to find out that they were indeed pregnant within the first month of their marriage. When little Francesca emerged a month before they expected, they realized that in fact she might have been conceived even before the wedding, though no one could be sure as Francesca was quite petite and it wasn't so unusual for a baby to be born a month early. Unlike Nicky she had silky dark hair, but she did have those big, gray eyes that marked her unmistakably as a Montoya.

She waved her chubby arms and her plump fingers danced dangerously near the elaborate icing. "I think she wants a slice." Vasco picked up the knife and handed it to Nicky. Now almost three, he took great pride in being an older brother and helping his baby sister.

"I'll cut her a big one, since it's her birthday." Guided by Vasco, Nicky plunged the knife into the rose-covered frosting with gusto. "And then I'll cut myself an even bigger one, because I'm older." He looked up with a toothy grin.

"What about us? We're even older." Vasco ruffled Nicky's blond hair.

"I think that means you have to save the biggest pieces of all for your aunties." Aunt Mari clapped her hands. "We're so old we don't even remember how many birthdays we've had."

Stella found it hard to remember how she'd coped without a large extended family to help. She still spent time every day working with the books in the library, and she and Mari had started to catalog the books, making several intriguing discoveries along the way. Her duties as queen were pretty light. Being a monarch in Montmajor mostly consisted of holding large parties and inviting everyone for miles around. Nice work if you could get it.

Vasco passed out the slices of cake, then lifted his glass. "A toast to our little princess." Francesca waved her sippy cup around with flair, giggling and slapping her other palm on the table. "Who will never have to leave Montmajor unless she wants to."

His words surprised Stella for a moment, then she remembered the strange ancient law that had driven Vasco from his homeland when he was still a boy.

"It's good to travel and see the world." Aunt Frida waved a forkful of cake in the air. "I spent three years touring Africa when I was in my twenties. And I ran a catering company in Paris for a while, too." The aunts— who did seem to have lived for several centuries—were constantly surprising her with their life stories. "But you always want to come back home to Montmajor."

"There's nowhere as peaceful," agreed Aunt Lilli.

"Or as beautiful," sighed Aunt Mari.

"Or with such good food," exclaimed Nicky, through a mouthful of cake.

"I have to agree." Stella smiled. "Though I think it's the people that make it so special. I don't know of anywhere on earth that's so quick to welcome strangers and make them feel like they've always lived here."

Vasco slid his arm around her waist. "Every now and then we have to venture into the outside world and find some more special people to come live here." He pressed a soft kiss to her cheek—which still tingled with excitement like it was the first time.

She sighed and smiled at her husband, and their growing extended family. "I'm glad you found us."

* * * * *

COMING NEXT MONTH

Available September 13, 2011

REQUEST YOUR FREE BOOKS!
2 FREE NOVELS PLUS 2 FREE GIFTS!

Harlequin® *Desire*

ALWAYS POWERFUL, PASSIONATE AND PROVOCATIVE

YES! Please send me 2 FREE Harlequin Desire® novels and my 2 FREE gifts (gifts are worth about $10). After receiving them, if I don't wish to receive any more books, I can return the shipping statement marked "cancel." If I don't cancel, I will receive 6 brand-new novels every month and be billed just $4.30 per book in the U.S. or $4.99 per book in Canada. That's a saving of at least 14% off the cover price! It's quite a bargain! Shipping and handling is just 50¢ per book in the U.S. and 75¢ per book in Canada.* I understand that accepting the 2 free books and gifts places me under no obligation to buy anything. I can always return a shipment and cancel at any time. Even if I never buy another book, the two free books and gifts are mine to keep forever.

225/326 HDN FEF3

Name _____ (PLEASE PRINT)

Address _____ Apt. #

City _____ State/Prov. _____ Zip/Postal Code

Signature (if under 18, a parent or guardian must sign)

Mail to the **Reader Service:**

IN U.S.A.: P.O. Box 1867, Buffalo, NY 14240-1867
IN CANADA: P.O. Box 609, Fort Erie, Ontario L2A 5X3

Not valid for current subscribers to Harlequin Desire books.

Want to try two free books from another line?
Call 1-800-873-8635 or visit www.ReaderService.com.

* Terms and prices subject to change without notice. Prices do not include applicable taxes. Sales tax applicable in N.Y. Canadian residents will be charged applicable taxes. Offer not valid in Quebec. This offer is limited to one order per household. All orders subject to credit approval. Credit or debit balances in a customer's account(s) may be offset by any other outstanding balance owed by or to the customer. Please allow 4 to 6 weeks for delivery. Offer available while quantities last.

Your Privacy—The Reader Service is committed to protecting your privacy. Our Privacy Policy is available online at www.ReaderService.com or upon request from the Reader Service.

We make a portion of our mailing list available to reputable third parties that offer products we believe may interest you. If you prefer that we not exchange your name with third parties, or if you wish to clarify or modify your communication preferences, please visit us at www.ReaderService.com/consumerschoice or write to us at Reader Service Preference Service, P.O. Box 9062, Buffalo, NY 14269. Include your complete name and address.

New York Times *and* USA TODAY *bestselling author*
Maya Banks presents a brand-new miniseries

PREGNANCY & PASSION

When four irresistible tycoons face
the consequences of temptation.

Book 1—ENTICED BY HIS FORGOTTEN LOVER

Available September 2011 from Harlequin® Desire®!

Rafael de Luca had been in bad situations before. A crowded ballroom could never make him sweat.

These people would never know that he had no memory of any of them.

He surveyed the party with grim tolerance, searching for the source of his unease.

At first his gaze flickered past her, but he yanked his attention back to a woman across the room. Her stare bored holes through him. Unflinching and steady, even when his eyes locked with hers.

Petite, even in heels, she had a creamy olive complexion. A wealth of inky-black curls cascaded over her shoulders and her eyes were equally dark.

She looked at him as if she'd already judged him and found him lacking. He'd never seen her before in his life. Or had he?

He cursed the gaping hole in his memory. He'd been diagnosed with selective amnesia after his accident four months ago. Which seemed like complete and utter bull. No one got amnesia except hysterical women in bad soap operas.

With a smile, he disengaged himself from the group

around him and made his way to the mystery woman.

She wasn't coy. She stared straight at him as he approached, her chin thrust upward in defiance.

"Excuse me, but have we met?" he asked in his smoothest voice.

His gaze moved over the generous swell of her breasts pushed up by the empire waist of her black cocktail dress.

When he glanced back up at her face, he saw fury in her eyes.

"Have we *met?*" Her voice was barely a whisper, but he felt each word like the crack of a whip.

Before he could process her response, she nailed him with a right hook. He stumbled back, holding his nose.

One of his guards stepped between Rafe and the woman, accidentally sending her to one knee. Her hand flew to the folds of her dress.

It was then, as she cupped her belly, that the realization hit him. She was pregnant.

Her eyes flashing, she turned and ran down the marble hallway.

Rafael ran after her. He burst from the hotel lobby, and saw two shoes sparkling in the moonlight, twinkling at him.

He blew out his breath in frustration and then shoved the pair of sparkly, ultrafeminine heels at his head of security.

"Find the woman who wore these shoes."

Will Rafael find his mystery woman?
Find out in Maya Banks's passionate new novel
ENTICED BY HIS FORGOTTEN LOVER
Available September 2011 from Harlequin® Desire®!

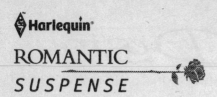

Harlequin®

ROMANTIC
SUSPENSE

NEW YORK TIMES BESTSELLING AUTHOR
RACHEL LEE

The Rescue Pilot

Time is running out…

Desperate to help her ailing sister, Rory is determined
to get Cait the necessary treatment to help her fight
a devastating disease. A cross-country trip turns into
a fight for survival in more ways than one when their plane
encounters trouble. Can Rory trust pilot Chase Dakota
with their lives, and possibly her heart?